DICKHEAD DAVE

GREAT RECIPEES FOR POT-HEADS LIVIN ON THERE OWN

Edited by Charmaine Snell

Copyright © 2019 DICKHEAD DAVE

Publisher: tredition, Hamburg, Germany

ISBN
Paperback: 978-3-7482-1950-7
eBook: 978-3-7482-1986-6

Printed on demand in many countries

"It's a holy plant given by God, the spirit of His son reincarnated in the soil."

A Rastafarian in Brixton

CONTENTS

THE RECIPEES

EPILOG 157

FANKS 'N' THAT

Cheers to Mad Mick McGregor, Rob The Knob, Pogostick Pogson and all my uvver mates wivout whom this book would never have got wrote. Cheers also to Paul 'Porky' Hamon for loanin me his keyboard, Scenic Sid for writin such a warm and genrous forwood, and special cheers to my beautiful daughter Charmaine for helpin wiv the spellin and grammer. I fuckin loves yer I do!

FORWOOD

by Scenic Sid

I've known Dickhead Dave for a number of years and can honestly say he's a complete and utter arsehole. In truth, there's very little to recommend him. He's a lazy, rude, arrogant piece of shite. He has no decency, loyalty or respect, no morals or scruples, as demonstrated when he tried to distribute pornographic material starring one of his relatives.

He treats women like dirt, sponges off his mates, steals from shops, and fucks anything with a pulse, including his brother's wife (fact), his best mate's mum (fact), and even a debauched one-off with Janet Street-Porter (hearsay). Apparently they met in a bar, got totally rat-arsed, then went back to hers where he rode her like an horse. Given the size of her nashers that sounds about right, but personally I don't believe it. I mean, why would a TV celeb have anything to do with a scruffy, smelly scumbag like Dave? On the other hand, why would anyone boast about pulling a bird that looks like she's escaped from the 3 o' clock at Goodwood? Either way, it don't bear thinking about.

The only good thing you might say about him is that he's not in the least bit aggressive. In fact, I'd go as far as to say that there isn't an aggressive bone in his body, but I think that's because he's always stoned.

I met him at a dealer's where we were both scoring some weed and was immediately impressed by his directness and candour. I mean, there aren't *many* blokes who'll give you a list of all their convictions within five minutes of meeting them. But Dave is one of those rare, open, frank individuals who not only recognise their failings but nobly admit to them with an honesty and integrity that borders on heroic. In short, he's a cunt and he knows it.

When he told me he was writing a book, I have to admit I pissed myself laughing as I didn't think he could write his own name, let alone a book. But having read it I must say I was actually quite impressed, though hardly relevant to myself as I don't live on my own and *certainly* don't need tips on how to cook. I share all the cooking and household chores with my fiancé Petunia. Even so, it's amazing that he started it and even more amazing that he finished it. It's about survival, which in his case is a bit of a miracle given that a lot of people want him dead.

So when he asked me to write a 'forwood', though initially reluctant, I finally agreed on the proviso it would be a no-holds-barred, unbiased critique with no interference from

Dave himself (not difficult as I don't think he can read). He agreed and here we are. And who knows, if he sells a few copies and gets some royalties, the tosser might even pay me back the five hundred he still owes me.

Good luck with it, Dave, may you continue to shag and prosper, and let's hope the police don't catch up with you in regards to the porn video of your granny that you tried to sell to the local vicar.

Sidney Dubois

Professional tree-surgeon and landscape designer with his own tools. For a quote call 07749 515031.

EDITOR'S NOTE

My dad is dyslexic. No doubt about it. It's never been diagnosed and hardly been relevant until now. I'd never seen him read a book or even write a card. But when he told me he'd written a cookery book and asked me to help him with it, my initial reaction, after almost dying of shock, was to oblige and assist in any way I could. I've always been good at English and fascinated by the written word. I also found it amazing and rather touching that he'd actually gone to all the trouble of borrowing a computer and written an entire book, whether good or bad, all by himself when he'd never even *seen* a keyboard before. It must have taken him weeks, possibly even months.

However, as I started to read it, I have to admit my heart sank and my literary high-horse started to gallop. It was *dreadful*! The spelling and grammar were *atrocious*! I soon realised that this was no *ordinary* case of illiteracy, this was something akin to a medical malfunction. There was absolutely *no* punctuation, he seemed incapable of differentiating between 'there', 'their' and 'they're', likewise 'your' and 'you're', 'threw' and 'through', and tended to spell words the way he heard them, for example 'masserkisstic', typical of dyslexics. Strangely, he'd sometimes get a word right then in the next sentence get the same word wrong again. Conversely, other more complicated words he actually spelt correctly, while *other* words were so unintelligible it was impossible to spellcheck them or find them in the dictionary. I amended and corrected everything the best way I could, adding commas and apostrophes etc. Then I suddenly had a change of heart. I stopped worrying about the grammatical errors and began to read it for what it was – a moving effort by an illiterate, dyslexic middle-aged man to make some sort of difference to someone's life. Everything else was superfluous. The spelling was immaterial. His voice and attitude were the important things.

Sometimes imperfection is perfect, and by trying to perfect imperfection you rob it of its impact and zest, a bit like adding a 90-piece orchestra to a track by LL Cool J.

I have therefore refrained from changing it beyond what I felt was completely necessary for you, the reader, to comprehend what the hell he's on about. For example: "To illystrait the poynt and for the perpurses of this book I actchilly kept a dairy ...." translates into "To illustrate the point and for the purposes of this book, I actually kept a diary ...." The rest is 'as it was wrote' apart from the punctuation marks, pronouns, adverbs, possessions and contractions which I felt were essential for clarity.

Happy deciphering, and I just hope and pray it doesn't all come back to bite him in the arse.

Charmaine Snell

PROLOG

People started callin me Dickhead Dave after a night out wiv some mates in the West End. Stormcloud Croucher had just got off his assault 'n' battery charge so we was havin a quick one to celebrate. This was around 12 noon, strait after the courtcase. Course one pint led to anuvver, then anuvver, wiv several spliffs and lines of charlie in the bog, and before I know it it's 11.30 at night, I'm off my face, and a desprate dash for the last train home looms.

I was livin in Watford at the time wiv the missus and her two kids, Daisy Mae and Romeo. Daisy Mae was four and quite sweet, but Romeo was a right little bastard. Six years old and built like a brick shithouse. He was already beatin up kids twice his age. He fort nuffin of punchin grown men in the bollocks. I once saw him bite an alsation who was quietly sniffin anuvver dog's arse - the poor fucker yelped in pain and ran off petrified (the dog, that is, not Romeo). Course I blame his muvva. Not only did she never tell him off, she hardly even *spoke* to him. She was too busy on her fuckin phone catchin up on all the latest showbiz gossip. She could tell you everyfin about Victoria fuckin Beckham and her silly bloody marriage to David, but fuck-all about politics or what was goin on in the world. Wars, famine, hurricanes, floods, and all she could talk about was Victoria's weight-loss and David's latest haircut.

Anyway, I didn't ring her coz I knew I'd get a rollockin. I was supposed to be back by six to babysit while she went to bingo wiv her best mate Beryl, the one with the itchy fanny. Apparently she had thrush or somefin. She'd scratch it in front of *anyone*, even complete strangers. She'd suddenly grimace and tear at it furiously wiv her nails, a mixture of pain and relish. I sometimes wondered what the inside of her nickers must have looked like but it was too horrible a fort to contemplate.

Anyway – where was I? – oh yeah! - I switched me phone off and carried on drinkin, assimilatin the bollockin I'd get when I finally returned.

I was in a great mood havin sold a bent Rolex to an American tourist. Immaculate it was, *and* it told the time. Three hundred beautiful smackers in the backpocket of me jeans. I was lookin good, feelin good, and *definitely* ready to party, prefrably wiv the barmaid wiv the big tits who'd bin eyein me up all night. A right little darlin she was, one o' them beautiful tarts, fit as fuck, wiv dyed blond hair, a low-cut top and a sexy mouth what you wanted to shove yer knob into the minute she opened it.

It was late November and fuckin freezin. Like a prat, I was only wearing a skimpy lightweight jacket coz it looked good wiv me jeans and t-shirt, and a brand new pair of Nike trainers what were the dg's bollocks. The overall effect was startlin. I was really rockin the look.

How the barmaid wiv the big tits didn't leep over the counter and make mad pashinate love to me was a mistery.

Anyway, it's suddenly 11.45 and I've got 18 minutes to get to Euston and catch the last train home. Stormcloud offered to put me up for the night but I declined. For a start he was legless and talking shite, but I'd also given his missus one whilst he was on remand in the Scrubs. So I decided to leg it back to Watford and face the music. There'd probably be a ruck, she might slap me a few times, but eventually she'd calm down and I might even get my leg over. I don't know about you but I really enjoy gettin my leg over after a row, especially if the bird is still mad at you and not speakin. For some reason I find you can fuck 'em harder, and they might even take it up the old cack-hatch if you're lucky. Some sort of masserkisstic revenge or somefin.

Anyway, I staggered to the tube, Leicester Square I fink it was, leapt onto an overcrowded train, got to Euston, sprinted from the underground to the platform and managed to jump on the last train home wiv only seconds to spare. To my delight it was fairly empty. I slumped on the seat, put my feet up, and promptly fell into a deep slumber. Obviously I was completely exhausted from drinking since lunchtime.

As the train rocked lullinly back 'n' forth, I started to have this dream about the barmaid wiv the big tits, the sort of dream you never wanna wake up from. She came allurinly towards me, took me by the hand and led me into the bog where she removed her top, then her bra, and proudly showed 'em off to me. They were the most beautiful tits I'd ever seen! Young, firm, big 'n' bouncy, wiv perfect rose-coloured nipples, not too dark, not too pail. She then pulled my head towards 'em and shoved 'em in my mouth, one at a time, allowin me to suck on 'em slowly and luxuriously. They filled my entire gob. Then she knelt, undid my jeans, placed my knob in the old cleavage, and proceeded to give me a tit wank, measured and sensuous. It was the best tit wank I'd ever had and seemed to go on forever. Then just as I was about to shoot my load she suddenly stopped, stood up again, dropped her nickers, turned and lent against one of the sinks with her fabulous arse pointin strait at me, and opened her legs invitinly. I was just about to stick it in her when she suddenly turned back to me and said ....

"Tickets, please!"

I was baffled. I stood for a moment purplexed. I couldn't work out what she meant. She must have read my forts coz she said it again.

"Tickets, please!"

I suddenly realised it couldn't be her coz it sounded like a man wiv an asian accent.

"Tickets, please!"

I slowly opened my eyes to see this little indian bloke, about four foot nuffin, wearin a conducter's uniform at least three sizes too big for him, standin in front of me wiv his ticket machine at the ready and an inane expression on his face.

"Wake up, please, I have to see your ticket!"

I was obviously a bit grumpy havin bin disterbed and my erotic dream interrupted.

"Can't you see I'm tired?" I snapped.

"I am very sorry, sir, but I need to see your ticket."

As luck would have it, I actually had one on me. I felt around in me pockets and handed it to him. He studied it carefully.

"I am very sorry, sir, but this is *not* a valid ticket. It only goes as far as Watford."

"Yeah, that's where I'm gettin off."

"But you've gone miles past Watford! You're only two stops from Milton Keynes! I must ask you to alight at the next station, please."

"Where's that?"

"Tring."

"*Tring*? Never fuckin heard of it!"

You know what he said?

"There's not much there but it's a very nice place to retire to."

I was speechless.

"Can't you let me go to Milton Keynes and catch the next train back to Watford?"

"There *are* no more trains, sir. It's gone one o' clock. And I cannot let you travel any further without a valid ticket, please."

Now I'm not genrally racist, some of my best mates are rasterfarians, but this little indian prick was really startin to get to me.

"Look here, Ghandi," I said, "I'm a British citizen. Why don't you fuck off back to Delhi and let us Brits live in peace?"

He looked offended then hurt.

"I must ask you to alight at the next stop, please, or I shall have to call the police."

I considered it for a moment coz the fort of a nice warm police cell seemed quite appealin. Then I remembered I was still wanted for several nonpayment of fairs so decided against it.

The train slowed down and came to a halt. I begrudginly stood up and immediately realised I still had a fuckin great hard-on from my dream. I fink he realised it an' all coz his eyes widened alarminly. I clenched my teeth and pointed at him.

"You'll be hearin from my lawyer! This is unfair treatment of an Englishman!"

I got off, turned back, and yelled at him.

"Hope you're happy, you official cunt!"

The doors closed and the train went off wiv the little indian bloke starin after me, wide-eyed and bemused.

I limped up the stairs, went outside the station, and suddenly I'm in the middle of a bleedin blizzard wiv heavy snow and gailforce winds eruptin all around me! No-one about, no cars, no taxis or buses. Completely fuckin deserted!

So there I am in a place I've never heard of, 1.15 in the mornin, wearin a lightweight summer jacket along wiv me Nikes, barely able to see in front of me, and not a bleedin clue which way Watford was.

I saw a road sign in the distance and trudged wearily towards it. The storm bit furiously into my face makin it feel like fuckin Siberia. Not that I've ever bin to China but you can fuckin imagine, can't yer?

I looked up and there it was – the harsh, horrible, cruel reality - **Watford 38 miles. 38 fuckin miles!** Everyfin sank, apart from my erection. A slow, torcherous, deaf-defyin journey stared me in the boat-race. I had no choice. I did me zip up and began trudgin threw the snow wiv the vague hope of meetin a bus or findin an hotel en-route.

The roads became more and more treacherus. Nuffin moved or stirred. I've bin cold before, I once shagged a bird in a storage freezer, but I'd NEVER felt a chill like this!

The street lamps what lit my path gradually subsided till I was walkin in complete darkness. My clothes was soaked and me Nikes were gettin ruined. Even me hard-on had started to diminish, thus diprivin me of the only bit of warmth I had. And I suddenly found myself prayin. Strait up, actually *prayin,* even though I don't believe in it coz if there was a God he'd legalize weed and he wouldn't have let a total prick like Donald Trump become president of the world. But on this occasion, wiv the snow and wind slammin my entire body, I prayed for him to help me (God, that is, not Donald Trump).

Help me, yer cunt! I yelled out in desperashun.

Suddenly I saw a light! No word of a lie, I saw a light in the distance glowin in the dark. For a moment I fort I might have died and left my body coz you hear about these fings, don't yer, about people snuffin it and seein a light. Then I realised I *couldn't* be dead uvverwise I wouldn't be so fuckin cold!

I walked slowly and evenly towards it, and to my astonishment a small hotel gradually came into view. Well, more like a guest house, but it didn't matter. It had its lights on and all I could hope for was that it was still open and there was a room.

I tried the door and amazinly it opened. I couldn't believe my luck. I went into a small reception area. A man was standing there, an old guy in his seventies, tall, thin, extremely pail, wearin pyjamas which I fort was a bit odd for a receptionist but I was too fuckin cold and tired to care. I managed to stop my teeth chatterin for long enuff to ask him if there were any rooms. He looked vacant for a moment then suddenly became animated, like he'd just come out of his muvva, and replied in a thick Scottish accent:

"Aye. Two hundred an' fifty a night, payable in advance."

A bit pricey, I fort, but I didn't have much choice.

"I'll take it!" I yelled excited, and reached into the backpocket of my jeans. Nuffin. I wasn't unduly concerned at first coz me hands were still numb. I felt again. The more I felt the more obvious it became that it weren't there. I tried me uvver pockets. Nuffin. The dosh had gone.

"What about a mobile?" he said. "Have ye no go a mobile ye can gi us as security?"

"Yeah – sure – no problem."

I felt in me pockets. Nuffin. I felt again. Nuffin. Gone. What the fuck had I bin doin in that pub?! All I had on me was a condom which I pulled out wivout finkin. The old geezer looked at it expressionless, then to my amazement took it off me and stuck it in the top pocket of his pyjamas.

What's an old cunt like that want wiv a condom? I remember fikin.

"What about yeez trainers?" he suddenly goes, all casual. "Gi us ya trainers as a deposit an' I'll let ye sleep oan that seat there." And he points to a chair a few feet from the reception desk.

Now under *normal* circumstances I might have bin a bit suspishus, but bare in mind I'd bin drinkin since lunchtime, fallen asleep on the train, gone miles past me stop, bin rudely awakened by a jobsworthy ticket inspector wiv a bad attitude, found myself in the middle of fuckin Tring in a howlin blizzard, walked for fuck nose how long, and here I am at least bein offered some shelter. I wasn't in any mood to argue. I took me trainers off and handed them to him.

"Have you got a blanket I can have?" I asked pathetically, still shiverin.

"I'll get ye one," he nodded, and turned and went up the stairs, his naff tarten slippers slowly disappearin from view.

I took off me soakin-wet jacket, flopped down on the seat, and almost instantly fell asleep again, hopin to return to the dream where I'm about to give the barmaid wiv the big tits one.

Suddenly, wivout warnin, I hear this loud gruff voice bearin down on me.

"Oi! You! What the hell do you fink you're doin!"

I open my eyes to see some sort of security guard, a short, squat, hard-lookin fucker wiv a shaven head and an intense snarl, holdin what looked like a club (the instrument for violence, not the chocolate bar).

"Get the fuck out of here before I use your face for baseball practice!" he yells.

"The receptionist told me I could stay the night," I muttered timidly.

"*Receptionist*?! *What* fuckin receptionist? We don't *have* a fuckin receptionist!"

"Yeah, he was standin here," I goes, like a lamb to the slaughter. "An old geezer in pyjamas. Scottish accent."

"You're fuckin delusional, mate! Now clear off before I punch yer teeth so far down yer throat you'll have to stick a toothbrush up yer arse to clean 'em!"

Panic and desperashun swept over me and struck me like a knife threw the heart.

"No! Please! Listen! You've gotta find him! You've gotta find the old geezer in pyjamas! He's gone off wiv me trainers! Brand new Nike trainers! Seventy fuckin quid they were! You've gotta search all the rooms and find him!"

"I don't have to do *nuffin,* pal!" he says, all full of himself. "Now get the fuck out of here before I turn your face into a McDonalds hamburger! The cheap sort what you get in Happy Meals!"

By now I'm brickin it coz he looks like he means it. And I started to cry. Strait up, I *litrally* started to cry. I just couldn't take no more.

"No! Please! I beg you! Don't send me out there! I'll die! I'll fuckin freeze to death!"

He looked at me, unmoved, then begrudginly reached behind the desk and brought out a cardboard box which he slammed down bad-temperedly on the counter. I stood up and had a look. There were a few books, somefin what looked misteriously like a tea cosy, a dirty old jumper full of holes that smelt like a tom cat had sprayed on it, and a pair of enormous hobnail boots.

"Right. Take what you want and fuck off! And don't let me see you here again!"

As I emerged back into the terrible and feroshus night wearin size 14 boots, a disgustin urine-stained jumper and a tea-cosy on my head, I seriously felt like an escaped mental patient who'd taken the wrong meds. Was I hallucinatin or was all this actually happenin?

I'd like to say that that was the end of it, that I somehow managed to leg it all the way back to Watford and return to the missus and her two horrible kids as though nuffin had happened and all was well. But life ain't like that.

By now the snow was so thick you couldn't tell the road from the pavement. I could have bin walkin *anywhere*. I suddenly see two headlights comin towards me. I fink it's a bus. I stick my hand out to stop it and the fuckin fing runs me over. Turns out to be a gravel dispenser. I fall backwards, hit my head on the road, and for a moment I fort I was a goner.

In the ambulance they removed the hobnail boots and discovered my feet had turned blue. At the hospital they put 'em in a foot bath and rapped me in tin foil. As the colour and feelin gradually returned to all my bits, fings started to look up. There was no internal bleedin, just a few superfishal cuts 'n' bruises, and the nurse what cleaned and bandaged 'em was a right little darlin. Annie her name was. She was twenty-two and shaggin one of the doctors, though I reckon she was secretly hankerin after a bit of S 'n' M coz she seemed to enjoy it every time I yelled.

When I could at last walk on me plates wivout assistance, they gave me some thick woolly socks and a pair of slippers to go home in. Long live the NHS!

I finally got in at midday to find the missus standin there lookin thundrous.

"Sorry, babe, I had a bit of an accident."

She suddenly grimaced.

"What's that fuckin smell?!" she shrieked, pullin an horrified expression.

I tell her it's a jumper from a lost property box in a guest house in Tring, then relay the whole sad, sorry story. I have to admit it *did* sound a bit dodgy, even though it was the truth.

"Don't fuckin lie to me!" she snapped. "You've bin fuckin my sister again!"

"No! No!" I pleaded. "I got lost in the snow! You *have* to believe me! I ain't gone *near* yer sister since I found out she has anal warts!"

But she weren't listenin.

"I want you of here! Now! I've had enuff! You're a no-good waste o' fuckin space! You don't work, you don't pay for nuffin, you're stoned the whole time ...."

"What's wrong with *that*?" I queried.

"You're a fuckin liability!" she shouted. "Get out! Get outa my fuckin flat and don't come back! I never wanna see your ugly fuckin face again!"

Her language was disgustin. Mouth like a fishwife's fanny.

"Are you on the blob?" I asked her, as though that would explain it.

"No, I'm *not* on the fuckin blob! I've just had enuff, and I want you out of here NOW!"

"But what about the kids?" I said pathetically.

She now looked incredulous.

"The *kids*? You *hate* the kids!"

"Nah, I don't hate Daisy Mae!" I protested. "I only hate Romeo and *everyone* hates him!"

But she weren't interested. She wanted me gone. I fort after a time she might calm down and soften, but she remained as unchangeable as Ray Winston's actin. And while I was in the bedroom packin my stuff, I heard her phonin everyone, includin all my mates, tellin 'em how I'd made up this cock 'n' bull story about fallin asleep on the train, gettin lost in the snow, and endin up in A 'n' E after gettin run over by a gravel dispenser. And that's when everyone started callin me Dickhead Dave.

Fuckin rich, innit? You lie threw yer teeth and they believe yer. You tell the truth for once and they fink you're bullshittin. Women are like life – you can't fuckin win!

I got on a train and went to Brighton. And that's how I came to write this book.

NEW BEGININS

This computer what Pogostick Pogson gave me ain't 'alf good! Every time it sees a word it likes it underlines it in red. Fuckin clever, right?!

FRESH START, FRESH FORTS

Ok. She's kicked you out, there's no goin back, you've gotta leave town and start again.

Don't panic! You've got this book!

You're sickened, devastated, depressed coz it was sort of alright where you were, you had a roof over yer head, food on the table, got a shag every now and then. She might have bin a bit of a dog but it felt familiar, safe, a place to hang yer hat and call home.

Don't worry! This book is here to help you.

But I've got no money! I here you cry. *I ain't got a job! Nowhere to live! I'm nearly out of puff! I'll never survive! I might as well be dead!*

Don't despair! This book will be your guide.

First of all, look on the bright side. It ain't so bad. It has its advantages. Fink of all the fings you can now do what you couldn't do before. Make a list. For example:

Sleep when you want, get up when you want, have a wank when you want, fart in bed, dive under the covers to smell it, piss all over the seat wivout her moanin, leave yer underpants on the floor wiv the skidmarks showin, pull a bird and bring her back, watch Babestation.

This is just a small example of all the benefits of bein on yer own. Ok, there's no-one to do the housework, the shoppin or the cookin, yer washin or yer ironin, but let's face it – she only cleaned up when she felt like it, shrunk all yer t-shirts, kept losing yer socks, hardly *ever* did the ironin, moaned when she had to do the shoppin, sulked when you didn't help her put it away, the food was probably rank, and the way she dished it up reminded you of a steamin hot cowpat. You're better off wivout her!

But I can't cook! I here you say. *The most I've ever done is heat up last night's dinner! I can't even boil an egg! I don't even know how to switch the fuckin gas on!*

Don't fret! This book will show you how.

Regard this book as your friend. I'm not only gonna show you how to cook, I'm gonna show you how to shop, get away wiv not workin, get money when you need it, keep yer stash topped up, virtually puff for free, not only survive but *prosper* and become totally self-suffishent!

We'll start off wiv small simple dishes like egg on toast, gradually advancin to more elabrate 3-course meals the likes of which you won't have got wiv no fuckin female unless you was married to Anthea Turner.

So let's get started. But first fings first. Before we get onto the cookin, we're gonna get yer life sorted. And the *first* fing you've gotta do is work out where you're gonna stay.

WHERE TO STAY WHEN YOU GET THROWN OUT

You need somewhere to hang out whilst you get yerself sorted. Here's where a mate comes in. But be careful who you choose. You'll still be reeling from bein thrown out, or even if you've left of yer own accordion yer head 'll be all over the shop, so don't ring the first cunt you fink of. CHOOSE CAREFULLY! What you *don't* wanna do is stay with some borin old fart who goes to bed early and whose missus resents you bein there (no offence, Scenic Sid). Women, for some reason, feel more threatened and protective of 'their space'. What you want is a pot-head who's single, who don't work, and can point you in the right direction for the job centre and benefits office. Remember - yer benefits 'll be fucked-up for a time coz of yer change of address, so you don't want some arsehole whose gonna charge you rent and insist you share the bills. You want someone who don't give a shit and is as out to lunch as you are!

That's why I went to Brighton. Mad Mick McGregor ticked all the boxes.

Not only was he a pot-head, he was actually a dealer, so there was always a constant supply of gear. He didn't live wiv a bird coz he liked his freedom and preferred fuckin a different one every night. He had plenty of dosh even though he lived like a dosser, and you knew you'd get to meet lots of new, interestin people who were constantly comin in and out to score weed and whatever else was goin. Most important of all, he didn't mind who crashed there. I once saw thirteen hell's angels kippin on his floor. It smelt like the inside of Ray Winston's speedos. But Mad Mick didn't give a fuck. He was a laidback dude who took life as it came. Right up my street!

However, there *were* a few drawbacks. Firstly, he played heavy metal full-blast, nonstop, 7 days a week. Eight in the mornin, after three hours kip, you'd suddenly here Def fuckin Leppard blarin out from his 2000 watt speakers. Then there were the screams comin from the bird he'd pulled the night before. What the fuck he did to 'em God only knows! He also had some strange theories and headbutted anyone who disagreed wiv him. For instance: Princess Diana faked her own death and is now workin in a brothel in Cairo; Michael Jackson used to give his pet monkey Bubbles blow-jobs which is why his skin turned pale, and Angelina Jolie is actually a man. Where he got his information from I'm not too sure, but if you questioned him about it he'd get really defensive and aggressive. "It's a fuckin fact!" is all he'd say. Or "*Everyone* knows that!" But the worst one of all was .... he hated gays. He'd hated 'em ever since one tried it on wiv him in Pentonville.

Now I don't know if you've ever bin to Brighton, but it's about as gay as you can get. It's the gayest place known to man! Every uvver person is gay! Everywhere you go, every pub, every club, every street, every AA meetin, every church service, *everyone's* gay. Gay policemen, gay traffic wardens, gay bus drivers. It's the gay capital of Europe, for christsake! So what the fuck Mad Mick was doin *livin* there is a mistery! And it wasn't like he tried to hide it.

"Fuck off, you fuckin benders!" he'd yell the minute he spotted one in his local.

"Take it up the arse, do yer, sweetie?" he'd suddenly ask a copper.

The threat of violence and arrest was never far away. So whilst I was grateful to him for puttin me up, his was definitely a place I had to get away from *fast*!

After three weeks I started lookin for somewhere of my own.

FINDIN A PLACE OF YER OWN

This may seem a bit dauntin at first since you've got no money till yer benefits come threw. But don't worry. There are ways round it. You may feel like you have no choice but believe me you do. Don't forget you'll eventually be gettin housin benefit, back-dated, and now that you're on yer own the council tax is also covered.

All councils have a cap (maximum amount of housin benefit, not that fing what women shove up there fannies to stop 'em gettin pregnant). But obviously it varies accordin to the property available. So Brighton, for instance, which has a high rental demand, will be more expensive than say Runcorn where only a fuckin nutter would wanna live. Course by the time you're readin this you'll probably be gettin Universal Credit. But the same rules apply.

Q: What is Universal Credit?

A: Fucked if I know.

In some ways what the housin lot give you is irrelephant.* Neither hear nor there. Start lookin *now*. Look at places for say £500 a month. Ok, it'll probably be a dump wiv cockroaches and mould on the walls, and you'll probably be sharin a bog wiv illegal immigrants. It don't matter! What's important is where it is in relation to the shops, in particular yer local supermarket. Don't worry what the fuckin furniture looks like, and if it *has* got cockroaches ignore 'em. Let's face it, you're on yer own again, what does it matter what kind of fuckin squalor you live in?

*I think he means irrelevant. Charmaine

CHOOSIN YER LOCATION

The most vital thing is where the supermarkets are, coz as a pot-head you don't wanna be walkin miles just for a loaf of bread. You'll be goin in and out of 'em a lot as you suddenly remember fings, so you need convenient local shops what sell *everyfin*. If it's a long trek you'll decide you can't be bovvered and you'll be forever runnin outa stuff. Choose the area, *then* find the flat/room/bedsit.

I settled on Kemptown, a loud, vibrant, colourful community full of gays, trannies, lesbos, diesel dykes, lipstick fags and cripples bang in the centre of Brighton.

It reminds you of Soho as you walk down St James Street wiv its bars, clubs and occasional sex-shop. It's noisy and crowded, lively and flangeboyant. It's close to the pier and the seafront, but its *main* attraction are the supermarkets. The Co-op, Morrisons and Sainsburys all wivin easy reach of each uvver. Pot-head heaven!

If you're choosin somewhere central like what I did the properties are likely to be more pricey. DONT WORRY ABOUT IT! Choose the location, *then* find the property. Worry about the rent later.

Havin chosen the location it's time to start lookin for a property. You're gonna need refrences and a deposit.

Refrences are easy. Just find a mate wiv his own business. It don't have to be much, window cleaner, plumber, locksmith, anyfin as long as they're self-employed wiv their own headed notepaper. Get 'em to say you've worked for 'em for ten years, earnin 20 grand a year, you're a good and reliable worker and bobs yer uncle.

I chose Scenic Sid for this particular task, tree feller and landscape gardner extrordinair, and a good mate as you can tell from his forwood.

He's fuckin useless at gardenin to be fair. He wouldn't know the difference between a weed and a dandelion. But it don't matter. He's got his own business and even his own business cards, and was happy to oblige for half a bag of homegrown and some ketamine.

The second one is what's known as a 'character' refrence. Any old fucker on the street 'll do. Just write it yerself, big yerself up, and get 'em to sign it.

So that's yer refrences sorted, now you need a deposit. This is slightly more problematic. But it's doable. *Everyfin's* doable.

Let's say you've found a place for £500 a month. You're gonna need a month's rent and a month's deposit in advance. That's a grand. But don't forget you're also gonna need beddin, cutlery, dishes, electrical goods etc. on top of that. All in all you're gonna need at *least* £2000. You don't have it. What you gonna do? Where are you gonna get it from?

There's one surefire way.

BRIBE THE EX

Don't be shy or pussylike about it. The bitch has kicked you out, you've gotta start again wiv nuffin, no money, no possessions, just the shirt on yer back. The *least* the cow can do is cough-up the deposit for yer flat/room/bedsit. You're not to worry where she gets it from, that's *her* fuckin problem! And remember: the bitch deserves everyfin she gets!

I'd bin wiv Delores for four years when she kicked me out. Four fuckin years! The revoltin Romeo was two when we first got togevver and she was already six months gone by anuvver bloke.

I met her in a fish 'n' chip shop. She was wiv her best mate Beryl, the one wiv the itchy fanny. I nicked one of her chips and she playfully slapped me. Later on she'd slap me harder and not so playfully, but for now I was immediately struck by her flirtatiousness and wit. She also had a great pair of knockers. We went back to hers and I gave her one. I have to say, hopefully wivout soundin too much like a perv, I'm very partial to bangin pregnant women. There's somefin about 'em. For a start the tits are all nice 'n' big 'n' juicy wiv all the milk, but I also *really* dig that bump. I find it a real turn-on. And, of course, the *best* fing is that you can fuck 'em up the dirt-box coz they're too big to lie on their back.

I moved in after about a month, watched her drop, and brought Daisy Mae up as if she was me own. Now I ask you - how many fuckin blokes would do a selfless fing like that? What kind of fuckin saint takes on anuvver man's kids what aren't his, actually *speaks* to 'em, gives 'em sweets and is generally nice to 'em, especially a little cunt like Romeo. A lesser man would have run. But not me. I stuck it out like the great guy I am. Ok, I admit I *did* have a go wiv her sister, but that was coz her boyfriend had gone off wiv her best friend and I felt I had to comfort her. Apart from that and a few quickies here and there, I was totally fuckin faithful and extremely good to her. I never hit her, raped her (apart from when she wanted me to), never stole off her (apart from the odd tenner for a pint), and never mentioned the fuckin loada weight she'd put on in the time since I'd met her (apart from in a row of course). Four fuckin years, then the cow kicks me out over somefin I never did!

So have no qualms about gettin money off 'em. The question is *how*.

As we all know, when it comes to money, women are as tight as Anthea Turner's arse-crack. They're impenitrable! You'd have more chance of shaggin an 80-year-old nun wiv a gungy minge (not that you'd want to). They're great at takin it off you, but not so good at givin it back. Here's where you've got to *really* fink hard and use yer nozzle.

What have you got on 'em? What do you know about 'em that they *definitely* don't want anyone else to know? What tantalising bit of information can you use to extort the money out of 'em? FINK! There *will* be somefin.

Maybe you've bin co-habitin but she never told the council. *That's* a good one. She could lose all her benefits and have to pay back a loada council tax. Maybe she ain't got a TV licence and could be in for a hefty fine or even a prison sentence if you report her. Easier for her to pay up. Or maybe you've got nude photos of her what you can threaten to put on Facebook or a revenge porn site. Maybe she's got one o' them fannies what farts while you're givin it one. It don't matter. Whatever it is, USE IT! (I *did* have some nude photos of Delores before I lost me phone but you couldn't see much to be honest. It was like lookin up the black hole of Calcutta. So I went for the fartin fanny one. She coughed up the next day.)

If you can fink of somefin better, like she's havin an affair wiv the vicar's wife, ask for more.

But that's blackmail! I hear you cry.

So fuckin what? MAN UP! This is war! It's about survival. And you need that fuckin deposit!

This computer's fuckin *mental*! I fink there's somefin wrong wiv it. Not only does it underline all the words what it likes in red, but it keeps addin a 'g' to everyfin. So, for example, 'shaggin' becomes 'shagging'. The same wiv 'comin', 'goin' and 'wankin'. It's drivin me nuts! I have to keep goin back and changin it, which is takin forever! It's a right head-fuck! There y' are – it's just done it again!

GETTIN A PLACE

Right. You've chosen the area, you've got yer deposit and yer refrences, it's time for you to find yer flat/room/bedsit.

Go to a lettin agent what specializes in short-term lets for students. They'll have plenty of property, mostly dumps, but they'll be affordable and they'll also be used to floaters (temperary tenants, not turds). Tell 'em you're only there for the day and you don't know the area. Wiv a bit of luck they'll drive you to the viewins. Always go for furnished. The furniture 'll be crap but you don't wanna have to start buyin yer own.

Always go there lookin smart, wear yer best gear and act like you're loaded. I actually wore me weddin 'n' funeral whistle, shirt and tie, wiv lashins of Au Savage. I looked and smelt the fuckin business, the sort of tenant any landlord would be pleased to have. And I wasn't *too* stoned. Just nicely zonked. If you go there too stoned they might not take you seriously.

"Are you interested in sharing?" was the first fing this woman asked me. I smiled but politely declined and explained I just needed a base whilst I looked somewhere to buy, so it didn't have to be too expensive or grand. Her ears immediately pricked up, she was suddenly all over me, and she starts showin me million pound properties on the seafront. Pretend you're interested. Study the details and act like you can afford it. Remember, gettin a place of yer own is all about lyin! NEVER tell them you're on benefits! Their attitude will change in seconds and they'll look at you like your an STD on legs.

We looked at three places, all in the Kemptown area. The young estate agent what drove me was wearin a really short mini-skirt what rose up as she was drivin, showin off her shapely, desirable legs, and I got a massive hard-on as we pulled off. It was a promising start.

The first place we looked at was an out-and-out hovel, dark as fuck, smell of damp, totally derrylicked* wiv a big fuckin hole in the wall! Even the estate agent looked embarrassed. "It needs a bit of work," she smiled apologetically. I fort of givin her one in the rubble but decided against it.

The second place was tiny, not enough room to swing a cat round (not that I've ever swung a cat, but I *did* shove an hamster up my arse once for a dare coz we'd heard that Richard Gere does it. The poor fucker leapt out immediately and promptly died on the carpet in front of me. I felt guilty for days!).

*I think he means derelict. Charmaine

It was one of the smallest places I'd ever seen! You could litrally lie in bed and have a wank wiv one hand and reach into the kitchen and fry an egg wiv the uvver. But it *did* have its own bathroom which was its main sellin point.

There was still a tenant in it, an old dear wiv one leg. She was goin into an old people's home coz she could no longer look after herself. I felt dead sorry for her.

"I hope you'll be as happy here as I've bin," she said sweetly.

I went into the bathroom to have a look and nearly jumped outa my skin - an artificial leg was sitting up in the bathtub! Now, I don't know about you, but I'm dead squeamish when it comes to deformities and artificial limbs an' that. I once shagged a bird who had a third nipple. Not only did I feel like spewin up, I wasn't sure which one to suck first.

We went to the third place and there it was – bingo! Right size, right rent, right location, and the minute we walked in, the second I saw it, I knew I'd found my new home.

Ok, it wasn't a palace, a few odd bits of furniture, a fold-down sofabed, a kitchen in the same room, bathroom on the landin, but as far as I was concerned it was the best fing since Keith Richards smoked his dad's ashes. Bang in the middle of Kemptown, just a coupla minutes from St James

Street, and there on the corner, at the end of the road, the best supermarket in the world – the Co-op!

If at all possible *always* get a flat/room/bedsit near a Co-op. They're a little more expensive but they're close and convenient, they sell virtually everyfin, the staff are always nice and friendly (more of that later) and best of all, they stay open till 11 every night. They also open at 8 in the mornin which is very handy if you're desprate for somefin like a pint of milk or some Branston pickle. You can still get the odd bargain and they do a very nice bottle of Chenin Blanc for £4.80.*

I *do* like a bottle of wine wiv my meals. Makes the grub taste better. Also helps you sleep better too. Trouble is, I'm now up to two bottles a night. That's on top of all the puff and the odd pint or two during the day. My innerds must be as fucked as Kylie Monogue's taste in men.

Anyway, back to the bedsit, and what I most liked about it, as well as bein close to the job centre was I could see myself gettin smashed there, crashin out there, gettin the munchies there, invitin my mates there, gettin the odd fuck there etc.

*All prices correct at the time of writin, Dec 2018.

It'll be the same for you. You'll know it when you see it.

ESSENSHULLS

Ok. You've got yer flat/room/bedsit. ITS TIME TO GO SHOPPIN!

Cheer up, dude. It don't have to be as borin as it sounds.

Get *completely* smashed! Get totally rat-arsed! Have even more spliffs than usual and visit every pub on the way there and on the way back. Maybe have a tab of ecky. Magic mushrooms are also good for this if you can get hold of 'em (Mad Mick McGregor always has a good supply).

Make it fun! You'll be shit-faced but it won't matter. Take this book wiv you so you don't forget what you've gone for and tick off all the items as you get 'em. (I wish *I'd* had this book when I was shoppin for essenshulls. I went to the shops three times, couldn't remember what I went for, and came back wiv six cans of lager).

You might have to make several trips, you might even have to get a bus or a taxi if the items are large or heavy. It don't matter. Enjoy the ride! Pretend you're a rock star! Get trolleyed each time you have to go, visit the pubs again, have a pint or a scotch in each one, and don't worry about the cost. I'm gonna tell you what to get and where to go to get it for the cheapest possible price. So chill. Have a laugh! Don't make it a chore. Imagine yerself sittin in yer flat/room/bedsit when you've got everyfin and you can relax and enjoy all yer mod-cons.

So here's the list of all yer essenshulls and where to get 'em.

First, for all your electrical goods, go to Argos.

Kettle £5.99

Toaster £7.99

Microwave £41.99

A Bush 49" flat-screen Smart TV wiv HDR £399.99.

You might find cheaper ones on special offer but make sure they've got freeview uvverwise you can't watch Babestation.

Total: £455.96

I worked that out on my mobile. But why the fuck do they always add 99p tot he price? Is it to *delibrately* confuse people on weed? I never met a pot-head yet who was any good at maths, though I do happen to know that Albert Einstein once took LSD.

Q: What if I can't afford a 49" flat-screen Smart TV wiv HDR? Won't a smaller one do?

A: No! You don't want some piddly little set what screws yer eyes up. You'll be watchin a lotta tele don't forget, so you want a decent size screen what you can immerse yerself in. You wanna be able to lie in bed wiv a late night snack and still see the tele wherever it might be in the room. Go no smaller than a 49". Rob The Knob has a 70". It's like bein in the fuckin Empire Leicester Sq! You're almost *inside* it wiv 'em. Great for watchin wildlife programmes and imaginin you're givin Rachel Riley one. Secondly, you *can* afford it! You should have allowed for this when you blackmailed yer ex. If not, go back and ask her for more.

Q: What if she refuses?

A: Say you'll tell all yer mates she's got a smelly fanny what she never washes. *That* usually works.

Q: By the way - how much is this book?

A: £8.99

For all yer plates, cups and glasses go to a pound shop (Poundland, Poundworld, Poundstretcher etc.) They stock everyfin and the amazin fing is most fings are a quid!

Half a dozen plates £6 (remember, the more you have the less you have to bovver wiv the washin-up)

Two or three cups £2-£3

Three or four serial bowls £3-£4

A couple of sideplates £2

One or two glasses £1-£2 (don't forget, you can nick some from all the pubs you've bin to)

Oven gloves (important) £1

A choppin board (likewise) £1

Bin liners £1

An egg cup £1

Total: £18-£21

Remember, you can also get all yer cleanin products there, though I personally didn't bovver as I wasn't plannin on doin any cleanin.

For all yer beddin, towels and bathroom stuff go to Primark. You won't find *anywhere* cheaper than Primark.

Double duvet £15

Double duvet cover wiv pillowcases to match £12

Bottom sheet £8

Matress protector for when you need a wee in the night £5

2 pillows £8

Towels (1 bathtowel, 2 handjobs) £10

Bathrobe for when you're entertainin £15

Loafer for yer back and scrotum £4

Total: £77

And, of course, don't forget they also do the cheapest socks, vests and underpants in the world. I know it's horrible to fink that they use asian slaves workin 18 hour days in places like Wolverhampton, but let's face it – they wouldn't have a fuckin job if people like us didn't go there. They'd be even *more* worse-off, starvin on the streets of Delhi. So let's do all those little tinted people a favour and shop at Primark. It's a godsend!

For all yer fryin pans and cookin utensils go to any of the leadin supermarkets (Asda, Aldi, Tescos etc.), *not* the fuckin Co-op coz whilst they've sussed that people have to eat, they ain't quite copped that they also have to cook it. All the uvvers do a wide range of kitchen products for a really low price. Morrisons, for example, do a good non-stick for about £7. And don't forget yer spatula!

For all yer cutlery – knives, forks, teaspoons etc – go to a greasy spoon and nick 'em.

So there you have it - all yer basic essenshulls for very little cost. You're bound to fink of more fings as we go along, but that's certainly enuff to get you started.

ESSENSHUL NOSH

Now that you've got yer essenshul goods, you now obviously need some essenshul nosh. Here are some of the must-have's along wiv my personal reccomendashuns.

Eggs (from a chicken)

Teabags (my favourite is PG Tips)

Coffee (gotta be Nescaff)

Ketchup (gotta be Heinz)

Salt (most supermarkets do their own but weirdly they're all made from tables)

Bacon (from a cow but you can also get it from a turkey)

Biscuits (Digestives coz they're great for dunkin)

Sugar (the white stuff, not that brown shit)

Bread (great for toast)

Branston pickle (small chunks)

Corn Flakes (what would pot-heads do wivout 'em?)

Baked beans (see page 115)

Butter (I favour Flora coz it lowers yer colestral which is very handy when you're wearin swimmin trunks)

Milk (vital for survival)

Tissues (for when you have a wank)

Bog-roll (for when you have a shit)

I'm sure you can fink of a lot more. But here's the clever bit. DON'T get it all at once! Do it in small spurts, gettin one or two items at a time ('a little a lot' as the Co-op would say). Go back 'n' forth to yer nearest supermarket as much and as often as possible.

Why? I here you ask.

Coz you wanna get to know the staff! The more you go in 'n' out, the more you'll get to know 'em and they'll get to know *you*. Smile, chat, charm 'em, make 'em laugh, call 'em by their name (that'll be on their staff badges). The nicer and friendlier you are the more pleasurable the experience and the less they'll suspect you of bein stoned out of yer bonce.

Especially get to know the security guard. They're the ones who stand there all stern an' serious wiv some sort of security guard uniform on. Always say hello to 'em. The poor fuckers are so starved of human contact they'll be flattered you've even bovvered to speak to 'em. Imagine standin there, day-in day-out, wiv nothing happenin, people ignorin you like you're a bad smell, dyin for someone to shoplift so you've got somefin to do. Ask 'em about their lives, their families. Show an interest and they'll be so overcome wiv gratitude they'll be yours for life.

The one at the Co-op was a black guy named Josef Bangu Dogboe, I kid you not. He turned out to be a really nice bloke wiv a friendly smile and a very interestin story. Apparently he was a prince in his native land of Zambia where he had nine wives and forty-eight kids. He'd come over to England to go to uni where he studied law and economics. Quite how he ended up as a security guard at the Co-op in Kemptown is a bit of a mistery. He never told me and I didn't ask. But the important fing was that over a period of time I completely gained his trust, to the point where it never occurred to him that I was an horrible, deceitful low-life who'd nick anyfin in the shop.

SURVIVIN

Ok. You've got yer flat/room/bedsit (I call mine an apartment coz it sounds posher). Unfortunately, you've now gotta pay for it. The rent, the bills, yer grub. In short, you've gotta survive wivout workin. How you gonna do it? You can't live on what the government gives you, *no-one* can. So you've gotta find ways.

Here's a few tips.

HOW TO SURVIVE WIVOUT GETTIN A JOB

1. BORROW OFF YER MATES.

Don't feel bad about it. That's what they're there for. Invite 'em round, make 'em a cuppa and roll 'em a spliff. Look a bit pathetic. Let 'em see your grotty surroundins. Make 'em feel sorry for you. Spread it on thick. Play the sympathy card. She kicked you out, it wasn't your fault, the cow took everyfin and left you with *nuffin*. You fink you're on the verge of a nervous breakdown. At the same time fill 'em with optymism that this is only temprorary, you've gone into partnership wiv Mad Mick and you're waitin on a big delivery. Could they lend you a bit to tide you over? Course you'll cut 'em in on the deal and any *future* deals. Remind 'em of all the nice fings you've done for 'em. And if you haven't done anyfin just make it up. How many meals you've bought 'em, how much dope you've given 'em, how many times you've bin there for 'em. Get 'em well stoned and eventually they'll cough up.

Q: What do I do if none of my mates have any money?

A: Get new mates.

2. INCREASE YER BENEFITS.

I'm assumin you're already on jobseekers and ESA (Employment and Support Allowance). You're schizoid, paranoid, and of course bi-polar (who isn't?). Maybe you're scared to go out, petrified of germs, terrified of pigeons. Maybe you've gotta walk on crutches for the rest of yer life coz you was run over by a council gravel dispenser (*that* should be worth a few bob when it finally comes threw).

All in all, you should already be on a fair wack, but you can still get more. For example: did you know you can get £70 a week if you're an alcoholic?* Strait up! 70 quid a week on top of all yer *uvver* benefits for bein a fuckin pisshead!

Alckeys can't simply stop drinkin uvverwise they might have an heart attack or a seazyer or somefin, so the government give you £70 a week to keep you drinkin to stop you from dyin. Fuckin laughable, innit!

Course you've gotta convince yer GP you're on five bottles of vodka a day but that shouldn't be too difficult. Just go in shakin violently and piss on the floor.

* Correct at the time of writin.

Also, as well as bein a manically depressed paranoid schizophrenic* you might also have somefin like M.E. (myalgic encephalomyelitis)** better known as chronic fatigue where you fall asleep the whole time and can't get outa bed coz you're so knackered (I fink I might actually have this one!). That bein the case, you might be entitled to a carer. That's anuvver £64.60 a week.*** Course, you don't actually *want* one or need one, you just get someone to say they'll do it then pocket the dosh and give 'em a small cut.

Now I'm not sayin all this can happen overnight. You might have to have a lotta tests and assessments, maybe see a few shrinks before you're diagnozed. But once you are, you're set for life.

*How on earth did Charmaine manage to spell all *that*?! (I keep telling him about spellcheck but he can't seem to grasp it. Charmaine)

**Told you she was a fuckin genius, didn't I?!

***Correct at the time of writin.

3. FLOG YER MEDS.

Course it goes wivout sayin that wiv all your disabilities you'll be on a lotta medication. Painkillers, steroids, antidepressants, uppers, downers, maybe even a bit of morphine for when you got run over by the gravel dispenser.

SELL 'em! You don't use em, so fuckin SELL 'em! You'll get a good price on any decent council estate. Chinkies especially, for whatever reason, seem to go in for 'em big time.

And guess what? It's perfectly legal! It ain't dealin! You're just helpin out a bruvver in pain.*

*Who the hell told him *that*?! Charmaine

4. ASK THE UNIVERSE

What a lot of people don't know about me is that I'm actually rather spiritual. No shit, I really am a spiritual kinda cunt when it fuckin comes down to it. Like I said, I don't fink there's a God uvverwise there wouldn't be such a fing as piles (my mum's suffered from 'em all her life, the size of fuckin grapes they are!). He'd also make sure that every bird was a nympho. But what I *do* believe is that there's some sort of universal intellygents what somehow picks up on yer forts and answers all yer needs.

For example: you want a shag. Ask the universe. Nine times out of ten some old bint 'll turn up whose hangin out for it. They might be in a pub, down a bar, or even standin on a street corner. I'm not sayin it'll be Scarlett Johansen or they'll even have their own teeth, but you'll *definitely* get yer leg over, and they might even take it up the poop-tube if you ask nicely (the universe, that is, not the old bint on the street corner).

It's the same wiv money. You need money? Ask the universe. I guarantee you'll find a tenner in the street. Or a mate 'll arrive outa the blue and lend you fifty.

This is a true story. I was once so pot noodled I couldn't even afford any puff. Seriously, I was down to my last few joints and smokin the dregs. I was *desprate*! You know what I did? I asked the universe, *that's* what I did! I asked, I pleaded, I begged! Suddenly, no word of a lie, I hear the roar of motorbikes outside, there's a knock on the door, and fuck me if it ain't my two best Scottish pals Wild Willie Saunders and Fudge McPherson!

They'd just bin to Amsterdam and come back with a full loada gear which they needed to stash somewhere whilst they went and got more. They gave me five hundred big ones and all the dope I could puff. Sorted!

And those sorta fings happen to me all the time. All you've gotta do is ask the universe and it'll magically manifest.

Q: How should I ask?

A: Say somefin like ....

Listen, mate, I didn't *ask* to be a pot-head but since I am you better fuckin cough up uvverwise I'm gonna fuckin lose it, punch someone in the mouth, and it ain't gonna be pretty! So fuckin do somefin before I go fuckin doo-lally!

5. FINK OUTSIDE THE BOX

Could you maybe get a record deal? Find an old rich sort and sponge off her? Sell an organ (the ones what keep you alive, not the sort you play). These are a few examples of finkin outside the box. Unlikely to happen, *definitely* off the wall, but you never know.

Rob The Knob once nicked a blind busker's money whilst he was playin his fiddle (the busker, that is, not Rob The Knob). I fink he came away wiv £3.76p. Now I don't necessarily condom* this, but this is another example of finkin outside the box.

*I think he means condone. *charmaine*

WHAT **NOT** TO DO TO GET MONEY

DON'T deal! If you deal you'll get a longer sentence if you're caught. Get it for yer mates, save some for yerself, and charge 'em a bit extra. That way you're virtually puffin for free and you'll only ever get done for possession.

Remember: if you're gonna break the law *always* consider the sentence before you do it. That way it won't come as too much of a shock when you go down for it.

DON'T get a job! It'll fuck up yer benefits!

One of my mates, Pogostick Pogson, also known as 'Pongy' coz of his feet, was an happy-go-lucky pot-head livin on his own. An ugly fucker wiv glasses, acne and the worst-smelling feet known to man, Pogostick was a sure fing to always be jobless and single. Athlete's foot, fungal toenails, bunions, corns, and a genuine medical condition called 'footsyitus' what made 'em sweat profusely.* Anyfin to do wiv feet, you name it Pogo had it. Course it didn't help that he never changed his socks and always wore plimsolls.

*It's actually called bromhidrosis. I looked it up on the internet. There's no such thing as 'footsyitus'. I think it's a word he made up coz he couldn't be bothered to research it. *Charmaine*

Did he never change his socks and always wear plimsolls coz of the footsyitus, or did he get footsyitus because he never never changed his socks and always wore plimsolls? It's a question even Jeremy Kyle might have trouble wiv.

Obviously wiv plates o' meat like that he couldn't work and spent most of his life on benefits. But he didn't mind. He was quite content sittin around all day gettin stoned, watchin daytime tele, and wankin over Loraine Kelly. Then one day it happened – he met a bird! Not just *any* bird, a fuckin parrot! Strait up, she looked just like a fuckin parrot wiv a big hook nose that seemed to cover her entire face and also serve as her mouth. Fuck me, she was ugly! You felt like feedin her Trill. And to crown it all her name was Polly. No shit, her name was *actually* Polly! But Pogostick fort she was the most beautiful fing on two claws. And once she got 'em into Pogo he was a changed man.

The first fing she did was to make him wash his feet and change his socks. Course, it didn't do any good coz of the footsyitus. They smelt as rotten as before he washed 'em.

The *second* fing was to try and make him respectable and get a job. And to everyone's amazement he ends up workin at Morrisons, minimum wage, 40 hours a week, wiv the possibility of overtime and a pension when he retired. They put him on the fish counter so customers wouldn't notice the smell.

Of course they immediately stopped all his benefits, including his ESA. By the time they'd taken a massive chunk for tax and national insurance he was worse off than before. He ended up workin 12 hour days, 7 days a week, just to stay afloat, and the poor fucker was so knackered he couldn't panda to Polly. He eventually handed in his notice and she dumped him. Poor old Pogo was heartbroken. Polly disappeared back to her cage, though not before Rob The Knob had given her one in the store cupboard of the pet shop where she worked. My God, that guy 'll fuck *anyfin*! He's only gotta *smell* an openin and he's like a deranged dog wiv two dicks.

It took ages for Pogo to get his benefits back and Jobseekers are forever up his arse to get anuvver job. He now has a nervous twitch and his plates o' meat smell worse than ever.

So DON'T get a job! It just ain't worth it! And remember – wivout people like us the cunts in work couldn't feel superior.

TIPS FOR A HAPPY LIFE

Always dunk yer biscuits (see next chapter 'What To Do If Yer Biscuit Falls In Yer Tea')

Always lick the plate (the best part of a meal and it saves on the washin-up)

Have a wank when you feel like it

Ketchup wiv everyfin

Don't get married

Eat what you want when you want

Don't go to the dentist

Live in the moment

Don't worry about money

Never save for a rainy day (it's rainin right now!)

Get excited about somefin, even if it's just the legs on 'Strictly Come Dancin'

Don't listen to negative people

Get out of it every night

Bang at least one black girl before you die

Never put an hamster up yer arse!

Don't fall asleep on the train and get lost in the snow!

Don't trust reality

Go to a Stones concert

Never be ashamed of yer genitals

Watch Babestation

Always have a spliff the minute you wake up. Make it the first fing you do. Don't wait. You'll immediately be back to where you were the night before, nicely zonked and removed from reality. Have a spliff before anyfin else. Great start to the day!

Be a dreamer. As a pot-head livin on yer own, it's your right, nay, your *duty* to be a dreamer. Wiv no-one else around to nag you and tell you what to do anymore, you can now dream away and be *anyfin* you want. As John Lennon said:

"She loves you, yeah, yeah, yeah!"

WHAT TO DO IF YER BISCUIT FALLS IN YER TEA

There is nuffin a pot-head likes more than dunkin his biscuit in his tea or coffee. It's one of the ultimate munchy experiences in life. However, there *is* an art to it.

Not long enuff and you won't get that sensual, soggy, biscuity taste mergin wiv the hot drink. *Too* long and it suddenly falls apart and goes plop in yer cup, sinkin to the bottom and creatin an horrible mushy mess.

There is no easy answer to this as the time you dunk it for varies from biscuit to biscuit. Digestives, for example, won't last much more than 3 seconds. Custard creams might take a bit longer, Hobnobs less. And if they're chocolate-sided you have to be even *more* careful. Yer tea or coffee could end up lookin like a baby's diper.

Then of course there's always the possibility that there's an hairline crack what you don't see till you dunk it and the fuckin fing immediately disintegrates.

If this happens DON'T panic! Grab a teaspoon and try to recue it before it sinks to the bottom and melts. You may just be lucky enuff to get it outa the cup before it's done too much damage. However, and I hate to say it, nine times out of ten it's a lost cause. By the time you've grabbed yer teaspoon and dredged it out, it's too late – it's destroyed yer drink and yer moment of pleasure. You have two choices:

1. Keep dredgin until there's only a bit left in the bottom, eat yer biscuit from the spoon and drink yer tea or coffee wiv bits in it, OR

2. Make anuvver cup. To be honest I favour this option, though sometimes lickin it from the spoon can be quite pleasant, especially if you're hammered. (Fuck me, if it ain't just happened again while I'm writin this!)

BABESTATION

In case you don't know, Babestation is a freeview channel where girls get their kit off and flash their assets in the hope that some sex-starved loser 'll ring up for a chat. Calls cost £2 a minute, plus £2 connection fee. For that you get a one-on-one conversation. You can ask 'em to do different poses, get 'em to talk dirty to you, or if you prefer just listen in whilst they talk dirty to someone else.

Rob The Knob actually called once and his fuckin phone bill went threw the roof! She kept him talkin for two hours!

But why fuckin pay for it when you can watch 'em doin it for free? The only difference is you can't hear what they're sayin coz they keep the sound down. All you can here is this horrible fuckin music. But let's face it, most of the time you want birds to shut up anyway. To my way of finkin, it's just as enjoyable watchin 'em writhe about, tryin to get you to call. They play wiv their manchesters, stroke the old Tom 'n' Jerry, get in all sorts of suggestive positions to try an' arouse the venerable meat 'n' two veg. Some of 'em stick their minge so close to the screen you can almost smell it.

Mostly they're just topless, but some of 'em are stark-bollock naked. However, you never get to see the actual Brans Hatch coz if you wanna see that you have to buy photos what are then sent to yer phone (three photos for

£1.50) and these are right up the old long-and-windin-road, no holds barred.

Again, Rob The Knob went for it and started doin it every night, endin up wiv about three hundred pictures of different fannies till he couldn't tell 'em apart. Needless to say his girlfriend at the time stumbled on 'em, asked him what they were, and he said they were holiday snaps. He ended up stayin at Mad Mick McGregor's.

Most of 'em are old dogs but occasionally you get an half-decent one what you wouldn't mind bangin if you was pissed and blindfolded. But the great fing is it's on all night and throughout the day, 24-7.

In some ways I prefer the daytime ones coz they have sexy gear on, really short mini-skirts what show their knickers and low-cut tops what reveal just enuff to get the old bobby dangler goin. After all, imagination is the muvva of invention, innit? Better to see up a bird's clouts and get a glimpse of the menu than a full-blown bankwet shoved in yer gob.

The best ones, of course, are the dirty old slags who don't give a fuck. There's one called Vidbeth who reaches new heights of sluttyness. Peroxide blonde hair wiv dark roots, a terrible figure, enormous floppy tits and a bulgin belly, a gigantic arse, she nevertheless shows it off like she's Emma

Watson. And you know what? She gets more phone calls than all the uvver girls put together! Coz men love dirty old slags, right? Always have and always will. Tell you what – I wish I was the fuckin cameraman!

Long live Babestation!

CHARMAINE

Before we finally move on, I'd just like to say a few words about my wonderful daughter Charmaine.

She's fifteen, a bit on the podgy side, but I reckon most of that's just puppy fat what she'll eventually lose. The main fing is she's a really nice girl wiv a lovely face, a warm and genrous personality, and brilliant bazookas. I tell you, whoever gets a tit wank from her in years to come is gonna be a lucky guy (hands off, Rob The Knob!).

But the most amazin fing about her is she's really, *really* clever, especially at spellin an' that. Where she gets it from is a fuckin mistery given her mum's as thick as shit and I never went to school.

She's the result of one o' them month-long shagfests where you're at it morning noon 'n' night wiv no fort for the consequences. I didn't use a johny coz they give me a headache and I assumed my swimmers were fucked. She wasn't on the pill but never said.

Her name was Rita, a right old scrubber but sexy as fuck, wiv a decent figure and a towerin libido. She was up for anyfin, anywhere, anytime, includin several sessions in the aforementioned storage freezer where Rob The Knob was an apprentice butcher. He'd sneek us in and we'd shag amongst the meat. I just wanted to see if it would stay up in extreme weather conditions and to my delight (and hers) it did.

It ended as fast as it began. Nine months later she turned up wiv this little bundle in a blanket and told me her name was Charmaine.

I looked at her and somefin amazin happened – I fell in love. Strait up, I took one look at her and fell in love wiv her. It had never happened to me before. I don't know where it come from.

And of all my illegal children*, she's the only one who's kept in touch.

I've watched her grow over the years and I can't tell you how proud I am of her. She's visited me a lot in Brighton, always turns down the offer of a spliff, didn't laugh when I told her I was writin a book, *encouraged* me even, and has spent long hours goin threw it, correctin all the spellin and punkchewasian.**

So I just wanna fank her for all she's done and tell her how much I appreciate everyfin she is and all that she will be.

I FUCKIN LOVES YER I DO!

Thanks, dad. I especially liked the bit about the brilliant bazookers. ☺ *Charmaine*

* I think he means illegitimate.

** Punctuation. *Charmaine*

Ok. You've got yer accommodation, your finances are sorted, you've got yer electrical goods, your cookin utensils, yer fryin pan, a bit of food in the fridge ....

IT'S TIME TO START COOKIN!

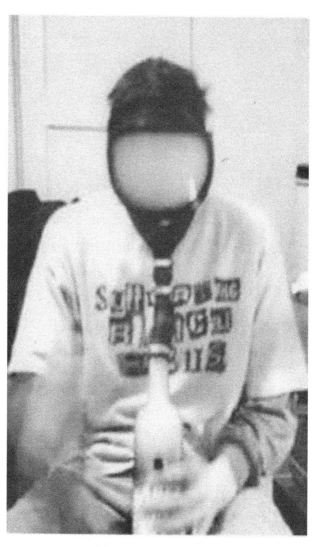

Me getting stoned

Scenic Sid and his fiance Petunia

Pogostick Pogson wiv somefin
coming out of his nose

Proof Albert Einstein once took LSD

Mad Mick McGregor wiv the munchies

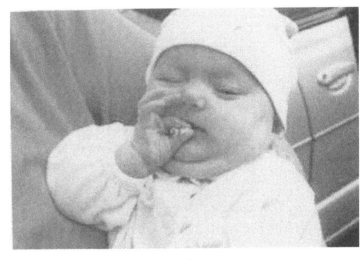

Me as a baby

My gran who starred in
the video what I made

Pogostick's ex-girlfrend Polly

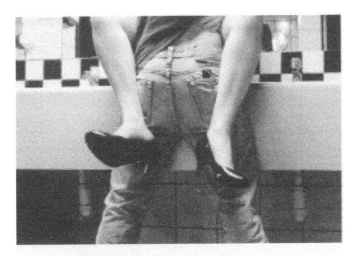

Rob The Knob on a night out

The vicar who I tried
to flog the video to

THE RECIPEES

So now, at last, we come to the recipees themselves. I've delibrately kept 'em seprate so you can refer to 'em again and again wivout havin to re-read this excellent and fort-provokin book.

Before we start, you need to know I've made a few assumpshuns.

One is that you've never cooked before in yer life. Your mum did it for you, then yer girlfriend, then yer first wife, followed by every uvver slapper you've ever shacked up wiv. It's perfectly feesible – women don't like blokes in the kitchen. It's their turf and they don't want you steelin their thunder. They assume you'll make a mess and they can do it better themselves. So you have no confidence and don't believe you can do it. IT'S BOLLOCKS! You CAN and you WILL! So start off by sayin these words:

I CAN DO THIS! I CAN DO <u>ANYFIN</u>! I'M A WHIZ IN THE KITCHEN! I'M A SUCCESS! I'M UNSTOPPABLE! I WILL BE A CELEBRITY MASTERCHEF! I WILL COOK FOR ROYALTY AND OPEN MY OWN CHAIN OF RESTERAUNTS!

Ok, that last one might be a bit ambishus but you get the drift.

I'm also assumin that you have a cooker what works wiv an oven and an hob. I'm assumin it's gas in which case the settins what I give you will be correct. But if it's electric you'll have to adjust the settins accordianly. So, for example, Gas Mark 5 is a moderate heat, Gas Mark 10 is high, Gas Mark 1 low, and so forth. I'm assumin you can read uvverwise you're fucked.

I won't be usin waits or measurements as I fink cookin is as much about *feel* as it is about the right amount of ingredients. I've seen cookery books what tell you to add 8 grams of butter, 2 ounces of flower etc. Fuck all that! The only grams and ounces I'm interested in are the ones my dealer uses to measure the weed and the charlie. Forget measurements. Smell it. *Feel* it!

Control the recipe, don't let the recipe control *you*.*

*What the hell is he on about?! charmaine

However, I *am* precise on the timins. When I say 3 mins I *mean* 3 mins. I don't mean 4 and I don't mean 2 – I mean 3! To this end you'll need a watch (a fake Rolex is fine) or even better a stopwatch.

Timin when you're cookin is *essenshul,* so even though you're in that beautiful, hazy, timeless zone what wacky backy so brilliantly delivers, you still need to concentrate on the timin.

Timin, timin, it's all about the timin!

Uvverwise yer food 'll be fucked or you might burn yer house down.

As I've done threwout this book, I've also tried to antipaste** any questions what you might have and answer 'em accordianly.**

**Anticipate and accordingly. charmaine

The last and final assumpshun is that you're totally wrecked when you attempt to cook 'em, uvverwise they won't make sense.

So wiv that in mind, let's start wiv somefin simple. Let's start wiv eggs.

RECIPEES FOR EGGS

Eggs. The most versatile of all vegetables. Forget that they come out of a chicken's arse. They're newtrishus, full of proteen, simple and tasty. Always have plenty of eggs in yer fridge. If you've got eggs and you know what to do wiv 'em, you'll never go hungry. You can boil 'em, fry 'em, scramble 'em, and if you're feelin *particularly* lazy you can put 'em in a cup and drink 'em. It ain't as horrible as it sounds. Once it's past yer gullet it actually tastes quite pleasant, and the great fing is that yer stomach feels full. It's what boxers have before a big fight. Two raw eggs in a cup every day and before you know it you'll have muscles like Rocky Balboa.

Talkin of which .... did you know the guy what wrote it, that Silvester Stallone cunt, did you know he used to be in porn films? Strait up, Rob The Knob brought round a DVD wiv him in it (Silvester Stallone, not Rob The Knob). 'Shut Your Mouth Before I Fuck It' I fink it was called. So there he is, all muscles and bulging biseps, about to give this bored housewife one, he takes off his gear, you're expectin to see thirteen inches of throbbin grissle, and there's this tiny little shlong what looks like a pickled gurkin. Made mine look *enormous* even when I was lost in the snow! Just goes to show, dunnit? You might have a six-pack but if you've got a small package there ain't a lot you can do about it – apart from write an Hollywood blockbuster and buy yerself a bigger one, of course.

Anyway, back to the recipees, and let's start wiv a nice easy one.

FRIED EGG ON TOAST

A delishus and simple light meal or snack, ideal for pot-heads learnin to cook. But be careful coz it's not as easy as it sounds. For a start you've gotta crack the egg and this can be tricky. Coz you want yer egg runny, right? You don't want it all hard like Ray Winston's performance in The Sweeney (am I the only fucker who sat threw that?!). You want it all nice 'n' runny so that when you stick yer knife 'n' fork in it, it runs all over yer plate and mingles wiv the ketchup to create that great munchy taste. If it's too hard it won't run and it won't be as good when you lick the plate.

So here's how to crack an egg.

Get a cup and tap yer egg *lightly* on the side, not too hard uvverwise you'll break yer yoke. The egg should crack. Turn yer crack UPWARDS towards you. This is EXTREMELY important! *Always* turn yer crack upwards and wait for the yoke to settle. Then simply open yer crack and pour it into yer cup. The egg should deposit nicely into the cup, *yoke entact*. Now you're ready to fry it.

How to fry an egg.

Don't laugh, this is serious shit! Yer egg needs to be *perfect*, not too hard, not too soft, and you *certainly* don't want it watery. It's totally down to how high yer heat is and the amount of oil you use.

Get yer fryin pan and put a load of cookin oil in it, and I mean *a load*. Don't stint. The more oil you use the less likely it is to stick to the pan.

Light yer hob, put yer frying pan on the hob, then IMMEDIATELY turn yer gas or electric down to MINIMUM. Leave it to heat up for a couple of minutes. While that's happenin you could stick yer kettle on and get yer cuppa prepared, and also yer toast, though you don't wanna make either of 'em too early as yer tea 'll get cold and yer toast 'll go wrinkly. You want everyfin to come together at the same time.

After a couple of minutes, get yer cup and gently pour yer egg into the fryin pan. Now leave it for about 7 mins, just enuff time to roll a spliff. Boil yer kettle and start yer toast. Light yer spliff, take a few deep drags, and imagine how proud you're gonna be when you finally cook somefin you can actually swallow.

Try to time it so that yer tea 'n' toast are both ready at the same time just before yer egg. Don't forget, yer toast also has to be buttered so allow a few more seconds for this.

Put the toast on yer plate, get yer spatula and slide yer egg strait from the pan onto the toast. There shouldn't be any sticky bits. Add lots of salt and ketchup and there you have it – the perfect fried egg on toast!

It *should* taste delishus (especially after yer spliff). But more importantly, you now know how to cook somefin you can actually eat.

Well done, me old mate! You should be proud and yer confidence should sore!

BOILED EGG 'N' SOLDIERS

Fill the kettle wiv water. Switch it on and boil it (the water, not the kettle). Once it's boiled pour it into yer saucepan. If it's a small saucepan (prefrible) fill it to the rim. Switch on yer hob, turn it to full wack, and bring it to the boil.

Now here's the clever bit – whilst yer water's comin back to the boil, which usually takes about a minute, get yer egg or eggs (I prefer two), put 'em on a spoon, then run 'em under the hot tap in yer sink. This'll get 'em used to the tempriture what they're about to go into (a bit like fingerin a bird before you bang her) and this should stop 'em from crackin. The *last* fing you want is yer eggs crackin and all that white stuff oozin out of 'em. The water looks like it's givin birth! To this end, turn yer saucepan down to a low heat as you put yer eggs in so they don't bang together or smack on the side of the saucepan. Then slowly turn yer hob back up to full heat and start timin yer egg as soon as it starts to re-boil. Timin here is of the essence.

Timin, timin, it's all about the timin!

You wanna give it five minutes, five minutes EXACTLY from start to finish. Any longer and yer egg 'll be hard. Any shorter and it'll be full of horrible watery stuff. FIVE MINUTES, no more no less.

Unlike yer *fried* egg, yer tea and toast will have to be ready *before* the five minutes is up, coz did you know that an egg continues to boil even after you've taken it out of the saucepan? Yes, it does. Fuckin amazin, innit? So make yer tea and spread yer toast a few minutes *before* the 5 mins is up. The same wiv yer plate and eggcup what I told you to get from the pound shop. Have everyfin prepared so that you can take yer eggs out and have 'em *immediately* so they don't get any harder.

Spread yer toast wiv butter (or in my case Flora) then cut it into small strips, narrow enuff to dip into yer egg. These are called 'soldiers'. When five minutes is up, turn yer gas off, take one of the eggs out and place it on the plate but NOT in the eggcup. Then take the uvver one out and put it in the eggcup. This is the one you're gonna eat first as it's bin in the saucepan longest. Remember, the *first* one will still be cookin whilst you're havin the *second* one so it's really important to get this right. Or is it the *first* one you have first coz the second one 'll still be cookin? No, it *has* to be the second one first coz if you have the *first* one first then the *second* one 'll still be cookin and the *first* one won't be as ready as the *second* one. Unless, of course, the second one is *already* ready in which case the *first* one ....

Is it me or is this fuckin complicated? Or am I just makin it more complicated than it actually is? What came first, the chicken or the egg? Why are we here? What is madness and who decides? Fuck me, this grass is strong!

Tap the egg wiv a teaspoon, take the top off the egg, add salt, dip yer soldiers in the yoke, and the first mouthful *should* be orgasmic, especially if you're smoking a spliff at the same time.

And there's yer second dish what you can cook all by yerself.

IS THERE NO STOPPIN THIS CUNT?!!!

SCRAMBLED EGGS

These are *really* difficult. Again, they have to be JUST RIGHT. Overdone and it'll taste like chewin a used condom, too runny and it'll be like goin down on a bird while she's havin a wee (come to fink of it, a lotta blokes like that). But if you get it right the rewards are *enormous*.

Two eggs in a bowl, stir 'em hard wiv a whisk, then pour 'em into yer saucepan.

Q: What if I don't have a whisk?

A: A fork is as good.

Q: Then what's the point of havin a whisker?

A: It's quicker and requires less welly. A bit walkin or catchin a bus.

Some people add a bit of milk but I personally fink this weekens the taste. Don't put oil or nuffin in the saucepan, just pour the whisked eggs strait in, then let it SLOWLY heat up on a low heat.

The trick is to keep stirrin all the time while it slowly goes from raw eggs to scrambled. It's fascinatin to watch, especially if you're on some slightly trippy shit as I am now (Amnesia 666).

You may have to attend to somefin else, like yer tea 'n' toast or yer neighbour havin an heart attack, but don't leave yer eggs alone for any length of time uvverwise they'll stick to the pan and you won't get as much.

Now I know I'm a fuckin jeanius and my cullinary skills are immense, but even *I* can't tell you how long they're gonna take or when they'll be ready. This is one of those times when you have to FEEL it, a bit like feelin when a bird is ready and you can shoot yer load. You just have to watch and keep stirrin till it *looks* like it wants to be eaten (a bit like yer girlfriend's minge).

Turn off yer hob and dish 'em up IMMEDIATELY coz, like yer boiled eggs, scrambled eggs continue to cook in the saucepan even after you've removed 'em from the hob.

Lots of salt 'n' ketchup and you've got yerself anuvver delishus meal/breakfast/snack what's great anytime of the day.

OMLET

Here's where we come onto somefin that could actually be a main meal and turn you into a coronary expert. Coz if you can make a good omlet, you can virtually make *anyfin*. The fuckin sky's the limit!

Crack 3 eggs into a bowl and stir vigerusly, prefribly wiv a whisk. At the same time turn the knob on the oven to grill and light it. This might be a bit dauntin at first, especially if you have to light it wiv a match, but remember – 'only the brave succeed' as Frank Bruno said just before he got the shit beaten out of him by Mike Tyson. Make sure yer rack is at the top of the oven ready for grillin.

Q: What if I don't have a whisk?

A: Haven't we just had this conversation? Fuck off back to the pound shop and get one, yer dozy prat, and stop gettin on my tits!

Put some oil into yer fryin pan, not too much not too little, light yer hob, put yer fryin pan on yer hob and heat the oil on a medium heat for 2-3 minutes. While yer oil's heatin, keep whiskin yer eggs till they look like some wanker who's froffin at the mouth.

Pour the eggs into yer fryin pan. There might be a sizzle. The eggs 'll spread all over and cover the pan. Get yer spatula and keep pushin the eggs away from the sides so that it stays loose and easy to remove (you'll know what I mean when you're doin it). DON'T overcook! Just a few minutes at the most. There might be some runny bits in the middle but it don't matter. That's where yer grill comes in. Simply lift the fryin pan, place it under the grill, the runny bits will continue to cook and the whole fing 'll begin to rise, a bit like a woman's tits in the bath which just happens to be one of my most favorite sites in all the world. Move the handle of the fryin pan about a bit to give it an even distribushun* of heat, and after about a minute or so remove it. It should slide easily from the pan onto the plate. Fold it in half, add a load of salt 'n' ketchup, and there you have it – yer first ever omlet!

*I think he means distribution. Charmaine

Do NOT underestimate this achievement! It's moneymental! From here you can go *anywhere*! You can add mushrooms, tomatoes, ham 'n' cheese, baked beans, peas, *anyfin!* Simply throw the ingrediants in wiv the egg and bobs yer uncle.

You can even start holdin dinner parties. *Everyone* loves an omlet!

BACON SANWICH

Bacon – the mainstay of students, dossers and pot-heads alike. There is *nuffin* like a bit o' bacon for makin you feel good and rejoicin in the fact that you're not a vegitarian. And what's the ultimate bacon experience? A bacon sanwich of course! Not only does it taste fantastic, it's also bin proven to lower yer colesteral.* So let's go for it!

Make sure you've got a loaf of bread what ain't gone moldy, remove two slices and place 'em on a plate. Pour a small amount of oil into yer fryin pan (cookin oil, not motor oil or 3-in-1. I should hve mentioned that earlier) and heat on a fairly high heat for about two minutes. Don't forget to light yer hob uvverwise yer bacon won't cook and you might gas yerself (this won't happen if you're electric).

While the oil's heatin up you might wanna butter yer bread. You might also wanna boil yer kettle, preferably wiv water in it, ready for a cuppa to go wiv it.

*Sorry, dad, but you're a complete and utter tosser! Charmaine

When the oil has heated, put three slices of bacon in yer fryin pan and cook for about 2-3 minutes (feel it, *feel* it!). Turn and cook for anuvver two (the uvver side never seems to take as long). *Never* turn it a third time as this will amputate the flavour. If you fancy it slightly crispy simply press the bacon against the fryin pan wiv yer spatula. You'll hear it sizzle. *Don't* use yer fingers like Pogostick Pogson who ended up in A 'n' E wiv third degree burns.

Take yer fryin pan off the hob, put the bacon on one of the slices, add a loada ketchup, put the uvver slice on top of it, cut it in 'alf, and there you have it – a delishus munchy bacon sanwich, great wiv a cuppa followed by a joint.

Course you can always toast the bread but I prefer it raw. It's one o' them satisfyin, holesome snacks what makes you feel all warm and content inside, so much so you may wanna go back to bed for a kip.

BAKED BEANS ON TOAST

Baked beans. The butt of so many jokes. From cowboy folklore to schoolboy rhymes such as:

Beans beans are good for yer heart

The more you eat the more you fart

The more you fart the better you feel

Beans beans for every meal!

A kid at school, BO Bonzie, came up wiv that.

BO Bonzie was a *genius* at fartin. He could fart on demand. Anytime, anywhere. Big ones, little ones, funny ones, sad ones, aggressive ones, cheeky ones, silent smelly ones. The list was endless. Brilliant for assembley and borin maths lessons. And he put all his success down to his love of baked beans. But in *my* experience they're no more wind-inducin than, say, four onion bhajis, a meatfeast pizza, a raw onion and a large bottle of coke. What's wrong wiv a good fartin session anyway? I for one thoroughly enjoy myself.

Anyway, regardless of the physical ramificashuns, beans are a worthy munchy snack and a great addishun to any fry-up (I reckermend a large tin coz you can re-heat the ones you don't eat later). But there's more to it than just openin the tin. For a start, you've gotta put 'em in a saucepan.

Q: What if I don't have a saucepan?

A: What do you mean, 'you don't have a saucepan'?! We've bin threw half a dozen fuckin recipees what require one! Why didn't you say somefin before?

Q: I didn't like to.

A: Why haven't you got one?

Q: You didn't tell me.

A: Fuck me, do I have to tell you *everyfin*? Ok, I forgot to put it in the 'essenshalls' and I can't be bowered to go back and stick it in there. I've got *enuff* on my plate havin to correct this poxy fuckin computer every five minutes! But I also expect you to use yer nozzle. *Everyone* needs a fuckin saucepan, for christsake! So go back to the pound shop and get one!

Q: How much will it cost?

A: A *quid*, yer div!

Right. So you've got yer baked beans in yer saucepan what you've now bought from the pound shop. Light yer hob and keep it on a low heat. Now here's the trick – stir 'em and *keep* stirrin 'em till they start to bubble a bit. Then turn yer hob down to the LOWEST POSSIBLE HEAT. This is called 'simmerin', a word I got from Nigella Lawson who I happen to be rather fond of. Nuffin wrong wiv a bit o' posh from time to time, especially if they're loaded an' endowed wiv those big homely bosoms what you can snuggle your entire face into. Wonderful on those cold wintry nights when an hot water bottle just don't quite cut it. And I bet she does an excellent roly-poly.

Anyway - where was I – oh yeah! While yer baked beans are simmerin, do yer toast and prepare yer tea but keep stirrin yer beans.

Q: How do I stir my beans at the same time as makin my tea and toast?

A: It's a question of time and motion. Heat down, bread in, stir. Toaster down, kettle on, stir. Get yer Flora ready, t-bag in cup, stir. Yer toast pops up, yer kettle boils, stir. Butter yer toast, stir, make yer tea, stir. Just stir every time you've got nuffin else to do. Yer beans 'll be nicely ready by the time yer tea and toast are done.

117

Now toast is the one fing I *can't* help you wiv coz it depends on the make of yer toaster and how you like it, so you'll have to adjust yer settins accordianly. Some people like it lightly toasted, some like it slightly burnt. I had a bird once who liked it almost black. Mind you, she was fuckin weird all round. She kept a pet python what she used to take to bed wiv her. I was goin down on her and the fuckin fing tried to crawl up my arse. It was one of the worst experiences of my life!

Put yer beans on yer toast, remembrin to put yer toast on a plate, and there it is – delishus baked beans on toast! Put the beans what you don't eat in a bowl and keep in the fridge for later. They're great in the microwave, 1-2 mins.

And remember:

Beans beans are good for yer heart

The more you eat the more you fart

The more you fart the better you feel

Beans beans for every meal!

A FRY-UP

Ok. You know how to do bacon, you know how to fry an egg, you now know how to heat up baked beans. Let's put 'em all together, add a few more ingrediants, and suddenly you've got yerself what is commonly known as A FRY-UP!

You'll probably be shittin yerself at the prospect of doin so many different fings at once but DON'T be! Wiv my help and guidance you'll be able to do a fry-up fit for a king (or even a queen if you live in Brighton). It's all about the timin, the amount of oil you use, and the settins on yer hob.

It can be as big or as small as you like dependin on the size of yer stomach, but let's go for a big one coz, a bit like minges, once you can do a big one you can certainly do a small one.

So we're gonna do: 2 eggs, 2 sausages, 3 rashers, a louda mushrooms, tomatoes, baked beans, 4 slices of toast and a cuppa.

Sound dauntin? Don't worry about it! If it goes wrong it goes wrong. So fuckin what? You'll get it right the next time.

And remember: enjoy yerself, make it fun! Cookin should *always* be FUN!

To that end, let's start wiv a brain teaser:

If one egg takes 10 mins from incepshun* (putting the oil in the pan) to dishin it up, how long will two eggs take?

If three rashers of bacon take 7 minutes from start to finish, how long will four rashers take?

I did this test wiv Pogostick Pogson. You know what he said? 20 mins for the eggs, 9.3 mins for the bacon. The fuckin dingbat! It's the fuckin *same*, yer twat! And to fink this is a bloke who could have gone to university if it hadn't bin for his feet. But when it comes to commonsense he's as thick as Ray Winston's beergut.

Anyway, back to the fry-up.

* I think he means conception. *Charmaine*

120

You'll need a second larger fryin pan for this coz you wanna keep yer eggs seprate. *Always* keep yer eggs seprate. I've seen some blokes do it all in the same pan, creatin an horrible oily mess. WRONG! It takes like slop, no care or fort gone into it. Fry-ups are like a dump – you need to take yer time to get the best out of 'em.

The trick is to get everyfin ready in advance. Crack yer eggs, turn on yer grill, boil yer kettle, put yer bread in the toaster, get yer Flora prepared etc. and make sure you've got yer spatula and stopwatch to hand.

We're gonna fry the eggs, grill the sausages, microwave the baked beans ....

You know what? Fuck it – forget it – I can't be bovvered. It's too fuckin complicated! Work it out for yerself. Better still, find a greasy spoon and let someone else do it for yer. For £6-£7 you can have a great gut-bustin, fatty feast and also nick some more cutlery to add to yer collection.

So far we haven't gone near the microwave, but all that's about to change.

MICROWAVE MEALS

Delishus, cheap, fast and easy (sounds like Delores). Just read the instruckshuns, bung it in the microwave, and about 5 mins later you've got yerself somefin akin to a school dinner. Fuckin lovely!

Most leadin supermarkets do a 'three for a fiver' deal, that's THREE evenin meals for the price of 5 Durex Pleasure Me Condoms. And the great fing is they're not too fillin, leavin plenty of room for the munchies (more on that in a minute).

They're pretty much the same store-to-store but I *especially* like the Co-op ones as they have a good variety and they're easy to nick.

My favourites are:

Beef casserole

Beef hotpot

Beef stew and dumplins

They all taste pretty much the same apart from the dumplins, but they're still fuckin lovely and EXTREMELY good for you!* You can also get a mean bangers 'n' mash.

The best news is you can eat 'em strait from the packagin thus savin on the washin-up, though I personally put 'em on a plate as it's better for lickin and I barely bovver wiv the washin up anyway. I just nick more plates. You *can* lick the container, but it tends to be more difficult as they have compartments and it can dribble on yer chin. It also tastes a bit plasticky. For my money, lickin the plate wins hands-down every time.

Note: Since the time of writin the fuckers have gone an' changed their prices. They're now 2 for £4. Whevver this is better than 3 for £5 I'm not too sure, but you now have to buy anuvver 2 coz if you only buy 1 it's an extra £2.68. So that's either 4 for £8 or 3 for £6.68. Confused? Imagine how a pot-head feels! You need bleedin' Rachel Riley to work it out for yer. Talkin of which .... I couldnt 'alf stick one up those short skirts what she wears on Countdown! Along wiv the bare legs and high heels, it's a wanker's dream.

*? charmaine

123

Thankyou, Rachel – thankyou for all the great times we've had together – thankyou from the heart of my scrotum. You are ravenous beyond belief, and long may you be in my spank-bank. Just wish they'd get rid of the fuckin contestants!

MUNCHY FOOD

A recent survey found that 9½ out of 10 pot-heads prefer munchy food to actual meals.

Everyone feels like a snack from time to time but only pot-heads get 'the munchies', that wonderful, overwhelmin, all-consumin desire for crap food full of fat, salt, sugar, hydrocarbrakes* and anyfin else what's bad for you. Chocolate, ice cream, peanuts, crisps, popcorn, biscuits, puddin, serial lashed wiv suar and milk, these are just a few of my faverite fings.

The munchies can hit anytime, anyplace. First fing in the mornin, last fing at night, in the middle of a dump, after a wank, on the bus, walkin round the Co-op. You spot a Mars bar and yer taste buds suddenly go ape-shit!

It's not about hunger, it's about *taste*. And, as wiv *everyfin* when you're stoned, your wants and needs are hightened.

* I think he means carbohydrates. *charmaine*

You've *got* to have peanut butter on toast, a bar of Cadbury's Whole Nut, you'd suddenly *kill* for a Co-op strawberry gateaux, fuck Teresa May for a packet of Hobnobs (yes, that's how desprate it can get!).

Be prepared. DON'T get cut short. Stock up. Fill yer cupboard wiv goodies. *Keep* it full. The last fing you want is to get the munchies and you ain't got nuffin. You'll end up pacin the floor, tearin your hair out, roamin the streets at 4 in the mornin in a desprate hunt for an all-night garage in order to buy an overpriced packet of crisps and a Kit-Kat. It's a piss-take what garages charge! So *always* have plenty of munchy food. Next to yer weed it's the most important must-have in a pot-head's life.

To illustrate the point and for the purposes of this book, I actually kept a diary for one week of my munchy intake. I've chosen Tuesday as a typical day.

DIARY OF A POT-HEAD WIV THE MUNCHIES

10am. Woke up, had a spliff, went back to bed.

12am. Woke up, had a spliff, went back to bed.

1pm. Woke up wiv the munchies. Had a bowl of Corn Flakes followed by 4 slices of toast 'n' marmite. Made a spliff and a cup o' PG Tips. Dunked 5 Digestive biscuits then eat a packet of Mini Cheddars. Anuvver spliff. Went back to bed.

3pm. Woke up. Watched Babestation. Had a wank and anuvver spliff. Got dressed, brushed the nashers, had anuvver bowl of Corn Flakes followed by last night's baked beans heated up in the microwave. Made a coffee, dunked 4 chocolate-sided Hobnobs, made anuvver spliff.

4pm. Wandered down to the Co-op for some milk. Bought a 6-pack of cheese 'n' onion crisps, 2 bottles of Chenin Blanc and 4 strawberry Cornettos for later, a large bar of Whole Nut, a multi-pack of Twix what were on special offer, and a bag of salted peanuts. Realised I didn't have enuff for the peanuts so shoved 'em in me pocket and forgot to pay. A bit risky as Josef the security guard wasn't there. Shared a joke wiv Daphne on the till. Suddenly felt like a pint but didn't have the dosh. Asked the universe. Found a pound coin in the street. Bought a scratch card. Won a tenner. Thanked the universe and went for a pint. Sat in the beer garden and had a spliff. Got the munchies and had a bag of cheese 'n' onion crisps. Called Mad Mick McGregor and asked him to join me coz I knew he'd turn up wiv some charlie. Ate the peanuts and rolled anuvver spliff while waitin. Ordered anuvver pint. Mad Mick turned up. Immediately had a line in the bog. Sat in the beer garden wiv Mad Mick and shared the spliff. He has a new theory and reckons he has proof – Jesus was an alien. No doubt about it. That explains the miracles and the reserection, not to mention the bit about him goin up to heaven. It's obvious – he went up in a UFO! Anuvver line in the bog. Suddenly off my face.

5.30pm. A couple of mincers enter the beer garden holdin hands. Mad Mick starts to kick off. I know the signs. "Wonder which one takes it up the arse?" Tell him I don't feel well and leg it.

5.45pm. Stagger in and realise I've forgotten the fuckin milk! After kickin the furniture and punchin myself in the face several times, which fuckin hurt, I come up wiv a brilliant plan (see page 134).

6pm. Have a spliff and a glass of wine. Suddenly hungry. Fancy somefin healthy and do myself a beef lasagna, 4 mins in the microwave. Add loads of salt and ketchup to make it taste better. Licked the plate, also the packagin. Poured anuvver glass of wine then had a large bowl of ice cream (sea salted caramel from the Co-op, fuckin luvly! Expensive though, £3.50 for a small tub. You can get the same fing for half the price at Aldi but I can't be bovvered – it's at least a 10 minute walk!)

7pm. Put my feet up, made a spliff, poured anuvver glass of wine and watched The One Show whilst suckin a Twix (you suck all the chocolate off first so that you're left wiv just the biscuity bit. Great munchy hits!). Fantasized over Alex Jones. Wondered what she wears in bed and if she talks dirty in Welsh. Realised I'd finished a whole bottle of wine and it's only just gone 7! Went to the fridge and discovered it was actually the bottle from last night so still had 2 full bottles left. Breathed a sigh of relief and praised myself for not bein an alcoholic. Suddenly got an urge for somefin savoury. Had anuvver bag of mini chedders.

9pm. Settle down to watch a movie on telly, The Amazin Spider-Man. Fantasize about Emma Stone whilst lickin a strawberry Cornetto. Wonder what colour her pubes are. Or maybe she shaves 'em, which I fink I prefer these days (you don't get hairs in yer mouth when you go down on 'em). Decide to have some toast 'n' marmite.

10pm. A brake for the news. Fantasize over Mary Nightingale whilst havin anuvver bowl of Corn Flakes. Wonder if she does blow-jobs (bet she does!).

10.30pm. Go to the cupboard wivout knowin what I fancy. Find an open packet of Doritos. Not sure how long they've bin there. Try one. Tastes alright, a bit stale but at least they ain't got mould on 'em. Film resumes. Find myself fantasizin over Sally Field who plays Spider-Man's aunty. Could I or couldnt I? I mean, she was a bit of a sort when she was young but it's a different story *now*. She's got to be at *least* 70! Decide I could. Finish the packet of Doritos. Open the second bottle of wine. Have some toast wiv peanut butter. Roll a spliff for bedtime. Suddenly crash-out on the sofa. Wake up at 3. Make a cup o' tea, roll anuvver spliff, dunk three more Hobnobs, 2 more slices of toast wiv peanut butter and watch Babestation for an hour. Pull down the sofa-bed, crawl under the covers, a quick wank then fall asleep for real. 4am.

Anuvver brilliant day!

Total munchy intake:

5 digestives, 8 slices of toast 'n' marmite, 7 chocolate-sided Hobnobs, 2 packets of mini chedders, 1 strawberry Cornetto, a double Twix bar, a bag of peanuts, a packet of cheese 'n' onion crisps, a bowl of ice cream, 3 bowls of Corn Flakes, 4 slices of toast wiv peanut butter and half a bag of Doritos.

On top of that – around 12-15 joints, 3 or 4 lines of charlie, 2 bottles of wine, 4 fantasies and 2 wanks.

Amazin how it all adds up, innit?

So keep yer munchy food topped up. Get somefin every time you go out. You won't regret it!

THE ULTIMATE MUNCHY SNACK

It's midnight. You're still hungry. You've had all the munchy food you can handle, yer stomach's fuller than Philip Schofield's bank account, but yer tastebuds are still goin gaga. You're still cravin that one last munchy hit before you go to bed. THIS IS FOR YOU!

You're gonna need some strong chedder, some Branston pickle, a sliced loaf and some thinly-sliced honey roast ham (£1.95 from the Co-op. It used to be a quid but their prices are now as erratic as Daniella Westbrook's nostrils).

Turn on yer grill. Put two slices of bread on yer grill pan and place it under the grill near the top. Keep an eye on it coz you don't want it to burn. No rollin a spliff or havin a wank while this is happenin – you've gotta keep yer eyes on the ball coz, unlike yer toaster, the bread ain't gonna just miraculously pop up by itself.

While yer bread's toastin, slice yer cheese, lots of it. The more the better. When yer bread looks like toast remove it, place it on yer work surface, turn the bread over and on one of the slices spread Branston pickle, then place the cheese on top. On the uvver one place the honey roast ham (2-3 slices), maybe wiv some mustard underneath (opshunal). Put both slices back under the grill and watch the cheese slowly melt. This is a beautiful site, especially when you're on the old Amnesia 666! The cheese starts to bubble then slowly drip like Angelina Jolie in the bath. The uvver slice may start to move around a bit, but this is quite normal. Some people reckon you shouldn't grill the ham but that's bollocks. It's perfectly fine. After all, it's already bin roasted. Just make sure it don't burn. You'll soon know if it starts smellin like a pig wiv a red hot poker shoved up its arse.

Q: What's that smell like?

A: A bit like shovin a red hot poker up yer *own* arse, I'd imagine.

The ham side may be done first. Simply remove it and put it on yer plate. Then when the cheese has melted to the point where it looks like Mount Etna havin an erupshun, take it out, add ketchup, put the two slices togevver, cut it in half, and there you have it. The ultimate late-night munchy snack, ideal for takin to bed and watchin Babestation wiv whilst happily munchin away.

Course it don't *have* to be honey roast ham, though that's my own personal choice. It can be anyfin you want - egg, bacon, fried tomatos, baked beans, a sausage. The *main* fing is the melted cheese wiv the Branston pickle underneath and the ketchup on top. Rob The Knob actually puts a kipper in his, but I reckon he's licked so much fanny his tastebuds are fucked.

MILK

You've bin to the Co-op, bought a loada crap, bin to the pub, come back pissed and forgotten the one fing you went for - milk (the only downside of bein a pot-head .... yer brain cells are diminishin at an alarmin rate!).

Oh no! Oh hell! It's *miles* back to the Co-op (2 mins in actuality but it *feels* like a trip to Syria). It's dark! It's rainin! The fort of goin out again is as appealin as Bobby Norris in a mankini. You can't borrow any from the uvver flats. The illegal immigrants downstairs never answer the door in case they're deported, the guy upstairs is a total recluse, and the gay couple in the basement are havin anuvver domestic. What you gonna do?

Don't panic! Here's where a bit of actin comes in.

Go outside, knock on a door, *any* door, look concerned and tell 'em you've found a stray hedgehog wanderin in the street and you've taken it home to look after it till the emergency hedgehog rescue squad arrive. It's lookin a bit the worse for wear and you wanna give it some milk to revive it (Scenic Sid reckons hedgehogs *love* milk). Unfortunately you've run out. Would they be so kind as to lend you some till tomorrow? They'll always say yes and nine times out of ten they'll give you enuff for a bowl of Corn Flakes and a cuppa in the mornin. The uvver great fing is they'll usually put it in a cup which is very handy for addin to yer collection.

If you see 'em again and they ask for their cup back, just say the hedgehog suddenly freaked out and smashed it.

CHIPS

What do pot-heads love to eat? CHIPS!

What do pot-heads want wiv every meal? CHIPS!

What goes wiv *anyfin*? Katie Price!

Apart from her. CHIPS!

What do pot-heads wake up for? A spliff and a wank!

Apart from that. The munchies!

After that. CHIPS!

There is only one sort of chips – and I don't mean the microwave jobs in the poncy packagin where you're lucky if you get half a dozen chips on yer plate – or the hit 'n' miss ones from yer local chippy. I'm talkin OVEN CHIPS! The food what changed the world!

Discovered by Stephen Hawkins when tryin to prove the theory of global warmin, oven chips have become the nation's number one life-saver and dinner essenshul. Fast, easy, convenient, full of proteen, and the good news is they don't *have* to be McCains what are fuckin expensive. Tescos, Morrisons, Asda, Lidl all now do their own cheaper versions, even the Co-op, though theirs taste funny. A bit like munchin a minge wiv salt on it.

The best ones are from Aldi, 80p for a large bag. 80 fuckin p! That's less than a Pleasure Me Ribbed And Dotted! And they're delishus! Strait up, I can't recommend 'em enuff. And of course, more than anyfin, they're unbelievably versytile. Coz once you can do oven chips you've immediately added at least anuvver 493 dishes to yer reppytwar!*

All you've gotta do is put somefin else in there wiv 'em and you've got yerself a full, heartwarmin, satisfyin main meal what even Anthea Turner would be proud to serve up. Fish fingers 'n' chips, pie 'n' chips, pizza 'n' chips, chicken kiev 'n' chips. These are just a few of the wonderful dishes you can now create.

A word of warnin about chicken kiev. Careful how you cut it coz it can suddenly squirt in yer face. It's happened to me several times, remindin me of a bird I met in Lemington Spar.

*I think he means repertoire. charmaine

You can also, of course, add somefin from the microwave. Nuffin wrong wiv lasagna 'n' chips. Or how about beef hotpot 'n' chips? Not to mention egg 'n' chips, bacon 'n' chips, sausage 'n' chips, egg bacon sausage 'n' chips, egg bacon sausage baked beans 'n' chips. The list goes on and on! The choice is limitless! You could even open yer own café though you'd have to get up before 12 (*fuck that!*).

The key to great oven chips is keepin 'em seprate and spreadin 'em out evenly. For this you'll need a big metal fing, I fink it's called an oven tray (£1 from the pound shop).

Simply switch on yer oven (gas mark 7), take yer oven chips outa the freezer, spread 'em on the tray so they don't overlap, roll a spliff while the oven warms up, then stick 'em in the oven for the allotted time (usually 20 mins). Some tell you to put 'em on the middle shelf, uvvers on the top, but in my experience it don't really matter. The important fing is that you turn 'em halfway threw cookin. Now when I say halfway, I *mean* halfway! That's 10 mins. Not 9, not 11, *10*! TEN MINUTES! Do you hear me? Uvverwise they'll get burnt or stick to the pan. *TEN!* I don't care how many joints you've had or how shit-faced you are. TEN!

Timin! Timin! It's all about the timin!

10 mins EXACTLY! Sorry to be so pediatric* but I told you I was hot on the timin, didn't I?

Then you take 'em out, turn 'em wiv yer spatula, makin sure you spread 'em out evenly again, then put 'em back in the oven to cook for *anuvver* 10. Not *9*, not 11, *10*! And in 20 mins, 20 mins EXACTLY, you've got yerself *perfect* oven chips.

Add salt 'n' ketchup for that ultimate chip experience.

Q: You keep talkin about 'timin'. Yet you also mentioned 'feelin it'. It sounds like a bit of a contradiction. Which one *is* it? Timin or feelin?

A: Fuck off, you arsehole! You're *really* startin to get on my fuckin nerves!

* I think he means pedantic. Charmaine

POSH NOSH

It's a Sunday and you fancy somefin speshal. May I suggest prawn cocktail to start, followed by a roast beef dinner-for-one?

The contrast in flavours is sensational, the delicasy of the prawns perfectly complimentin the tuff, rugged outdoor flavour of the beef.

Dinners-for-one have bin around as long as Ann Widdecombe's fanny. But the good news is they no longer have to be Captain Birds-Eye as most leadin supermarkets now do their own (apart from the fuckin Co-op of course!).

As well as the beef 'n' gravy you also get peas 'n' carrots, roast potatoes, and a stunnin yorkshire puddin. Yer classical British Sunday roast. And it only takes about 7-8 mins in the microwave.

Prices vary. £2.29 in Aldi, £1.69 in Iceland, and Morrisons even do some for a quid, though you get these greedy fuckers what grab a dozen at a time, leavin none for the rest of us (I *hate* selfish cunts like that! They should be prostituted*, have their fuckin eyes 'n' tongue ripped out, both their hands chopped off and shoved up their fuckin anus!). Captain Birds Eye ones are about £3 but still terrific value for money.

Prawn cocktails also vary dramatically in price. They used to be universally a quid, but now they've gone up as prawns have become one of the most popular pets on the planet. £1.69 in the Co-op, £2.40 in Tescos, and a woppin £3 in Marks, but only ponces shop there.

Prawn cocktail is a great starter and always adds a speshal somefin to every meal. You can have it wiv lettuce or even a poofy avocardo, but I prefer it on its own strait from the carton. It's the cocktail sauce what gives it its unique zest. Fuck nose what's in it but who cares? It beats pelican's penis any day!

So there you have it, a delishus posh meal for under a fiver, ready in minutes. It's what I call airoplane food, you know, the sort they dish up on long flights (I once went to Benidorm for 'Lippy' Lipton's stag-do).

*Does he mean prosecuted? Charmaine

You can eat all of it strait from the packagin, savin on the washin-up, and better still pretend you're on yer way to some hot, exotic locashun bein served by an attractive air hostess wiv unbelievably long legs what fancies you rotten and is gonna toss you off in the toilet.

Like I said – be a dreamer.

CHILLY CON CARNE

For those of you who love Spanish food, an exotic and excitin dish what's bound to tittylate yer tastebuds.

The Co-op do a tin for £1.75 (correct at the time of writin, but the fuckers change their prices more often than Princess Eugenie changes her nickers).

Just put it in a saucepan and heat it up. It tastes like shit but fills a gap between spliffs.

ROAST CHICKEN

You've met someone. She's gorgeous, sexy, classy, an absolute babe. You can't believe yer luck. You've invited her round for dinner and she's said yes. You're *desperate* to make an impression. What you gonna cook? It needs to be stylish wivout bein fussy, posh wivout bein poncy, fancy wivout bein flash.

Chicken. You can't go wrong wiv chicken (unless of course she's one o' them fuckin vegans, in which case forget it. You'll never get past her nut roast 'n' lentils).

I'm talkin *real* chicken, *proper* chicken, suckulent roast chicken what you bung in the oven and have wiv all the trimmins – roast potatoes, homemade stuffin, honey and mustard gravy, sautéed leeks, caramelised carrots (fanks for that, Charmaine). It ain't easy, you'll be a nervous reck, but the results 'll be worth it.

Wiv the assistance of my amazin daughter who has kindly written down all the ingredients and recipees for each accompanyin dish, we're gonna deliver a meal that'll knock yer tits off. If you don't get yer leg over after this, you might as well jack it in and become like Cliff Richard.

Firstly, you'll need a chicken. Make it a big one coz it looks better. A little scrawny one will send the wrong message, like you don't work and you're a bit of a layabout. So we're lookin at a 2-3 kg bird what'll set you back around £6-£7. This 'll look impressive and also do you for the rest of the week.

Q: What if I can't afford it? What if me benefits haven't come threw? Or me ESA is suspended? I've already invited her round, what should I do? Should I cancel?

A: No! Don't cancel. *Never* cancel! It'll put her off and give her more time to fink about it and she might change her mind.

Q: So what should I do?

A: Nick it.

Q: Eh?

A: Nick it. Nick a chicken. A hole chicken. Not half a chicken or a leg – a *hole* one. Coz, diversely, the bigger it is the more likely you are to get away wiv it.

Now, as you know, I don't really approve of nickin from shops, apart from the odd packet of Walkers Sensations and uvver small items (the Thai Sweet Chilli flavour are especially yummy) coz it's a bit like robin Peter to pay Paul. They simply put their prices up which affects us all. But there *are* times when it's essenshul. You have no choice. I blame the government. If the fuckers upped our benefits you wouldn't have this problem. I'd like to see Teresa fuckin May and her bland, borin, good-for-nuffin fuckin husband survive on what they give us (I mean, what does he actually *do,* apart from make her cups of cocoa?!).

This is one o' those times. So we're gonna steal it. It takes balls – but here's how you do it.

HOW TO STEAL A CHICKEN

Ok. Listen up. Pay attenshun coz you can only do this once. Here's where all yer actin skills and months of hard work gettin to know the staff pays off ....

Make sure you're wearin a jacket wiv a zip (a bomber jacket is ideal for this). Go to yer local supermarket, in my case the Co-op. Make sure your mate the security guard is there, in my case Josef. This is *very* important coz if the security guard is there then Daphne behind the till and all the uvver staff won't be bovverin. They'll be leavin it all up to Josef. Josef won't suspect nuffin coz you're his mate.

Enter normally. Smile and say hello, as per normal. Chat to Josef, ask him how his wives are etc., as per normal. That's the key word here – *normal*.

Pick up a basket and stroll lesherly down the aisle, pickin up random bits, and slowly make your way to the meat sexshun what is usually at the bottom of the store. Make sure yer zip is done up. Stop and casually study the chickens. Pick the *largest* one up and pretend to read the label. Then calmly and unhurriedly put the chicken in yer jacket and hold it there wiv one arm whilst holdin the basket wiv the uvver. Turn and walk *normally* to the tills. Then, just as you get there, suddenly let out an enormous scream, drop the basket so that all the items go everywhere, and fall to yer knees clutchin yer stomach in terrible agony like you're a woman about to give birth (it'll help if you've watched Call The Midwife). Be as loud and as animated as possible. By drawin attenshun to yerself, you'll be drawin attenshun *away* from the chicken. Writhe around but DON'T overdo it and roll all over the shop as the chicken might become exposed or, worse still, get squashed. The important fing is to keep clutchin yer stomach. The entire store will rush to your aid. They'll probably ask you if you need an ambulance. Simply shake yer head and, threw gritted teeth, say you fink it's grumbling appendix what you've had before. Then get to your feet and half-crawl, half-limp out of the shop, yer face still contorted in agony.

DON'T suddenly run when you get outside as someone may be watchin. Continue to walk in excrushiatin pain all the way up the road till you're back inside yer apartment. And *that's* how you steal a chicken.

COOKIN IT

So you've made it home. Yer chicken 'll probably be a bit battered wiv all the writhin around, so the first fing is to bash it back into shape.

Turn on yer oven, gas mark 6, and while it's warmin plonk the chicken in yer oven tray and smuvver it wiv salt 'n' oil. This is really important. The more oil the better. Then rub it slowly in like you're givin Carol Vorderman a massage.

Q: Why Carol Vorderman?

A: I dunno, she just came into my forts.

Make sure there's still plenty of oil floatin around in the bottom of the tray. Then when yer oven is nicely hot, put the chicken on the middle shelf and begin yer timin. How long it takes depends on the weight of yer bird what you'll find on the packagin. It's 40 mins per kg, plus anuvver 20 mins on top of that. So if yer chicken is 3 kgs, that's 2 hours in all. But that's a *big* fuckin bird! A bird that size you could dress up and pretend it's Gemma Collins. It's more likely to be, for example, 2.15 kgs which is …. which is …. finkin about it, that's probably why I started finkin about Carol Vorderman. Amazin how one fort leads to anuvver, innit? I'm sure you can work it out for yerself wiv a pen and paper or the calculater on yer mobile.

Q: What's Carol Vorderman got to do wiv the time it takes to roast a chicken?

A: Coz she's good at Maths, yer twat!

Once yer chicken is in the oven, take it out every 15-20 mins to 'baste' it. That's anuvver classy chef word what I learnt from Nigella Lawson on one of her cookery programmes. I was havin a wank at the time, but the word 'baste' somehow stuck wiv me. It's where you get a big spoon, gather up the oil from the pan, and pour it over yer bird to keep it moist (I occasionally did this wiv Delores). Then you put it back in the oven till it's time to 'baste' it again. Remember to use yer oven gloves, uvverwise you'll end up in A 'n' E like Pogostick Pogson and a wank 'll be outa the question.

While yer chicken is roastin, prepare all yer vegetables. Peel yer potatos, boil yer carrots, chop yer leaks, all the while keepin an eye on the clock as timin is of the essence. Remember, it's 40 mins per kg, plus 20 mins on top.

Q: At the beginning you said you wouldn't be using weights or measurements, yet here you are doin exactly that. I'm a little confused. Is it 'feel', 'timin', weights or measurements? I really fink you need to make your mind up.

A: Look here, you cunt! I'll fuckin hit you in a minute, you arrogant arsehole! Who do you fink you are? If you're so fuckin clever why don't *you* write the fuckin book! Go on, I *dare* yer! You wouldn't complete a single page, you ponced-up prick! Wait a minute .... wait a minute .... it's me. Oh my god, I'm fightin wiv meself! Oh hell! It must be livin on my own! I must be goin one fry short of a Happy Meal! And why can't I stop writin? Maybe it's all the skunk! That last lot was the strongest yet! Or maybe it's all the charlie I had today wiv Mad Mick. Wait a minute .... he also gave me a pill.

What the fuck *was* it? He didn't say I didnt ask I just took it. OH FUCK! Perhaps I'm hallucenatin! Perhaps I've given birth to a double!

Six, five four .... ground control to major Tom .... it's ok .... I am in complete command of my assets! Three, two, one .... hot .... hot .... it's gettin hot .... gettin hotter .... oh god, it's *so* hot! .... I can't stop writin .... why is it so hot? .... wait a minute .... fuck me, the kitchen's on fire!

KITCHEN DISASTERS

There comes a time when every cook has a kitchen disaster. Yer yoke brakes, yer bacon burns, yer chips shrivel up, yer oven gloves catch light and you have to evacuate the buildin. Don't worry about it! It happens to the best chefs. Learn from it and move on. And remember – the more disasters you have *now*, the more successes you'll have later. Gordon Ramsey apparently burnt down 8 kitchens, 4 resteraunts and his dad's garden shed before landin his first TV series.

Q: How did your date go?

A: She went off wiv one o' the firemen.

FINAL FORTS

And there you have it. You're now a cook. If nuffin else you can whip up an omlet, a bacon sarnie, a posh roast beef dinner-for-one. We've covered a lotta ground, everyfin from eggs to roast chicken, wiv plenty of munchy food thrown in. You're set to go.

I hope you've learnt somefin. And I hope you now go onto create yer own great dishes. Be inventive, be advencherus, take risks. 'With big risks come big rewards' as Sadam Hussein once said. Just throw everyfin in there and see what happens.

Cookin is like sex – the more you do it the easier it becomes, a bit like rollin a joint. It'll soon be second nature. Cookin is about *confidence*. So don't let no fuckin woman put you down and say you can't do it coz you *can*. Don't listen when they tell you you're useless and can't do nuffin. They just wanna be in control.

Now before anyone finks I'm a massausagenist*, I'd just like to clarify somefin. I LOVE WOMEN! I FUCKIN ADORE 'EM! There's nuffin like 'em for gettin yer leg over. I just don't like it when they get all full of 'emselves, take a bloke for granted, and act like they fuckin own him. After all, Adam came before Eve, didn't he? It was only when God looked down and saw how frustrated Adam was that he decided to create Eve. And what a fuckin disaster *that* was!

As you may have gathered, I've now changed my mind and believe that there *is* a God after all, uvverwise there wouldn't be somefin as beautiful as my daughter Charmaine. I was watchin her the uvver night while she was helpin me wiv this book, and there was a light comin out of her. Strait up, a fuckin light! 'Fuck me,' I fort, 'she's a fuckin angel!' And you can't have angels wivout a God, can yer? Admittedly I *had* taken a tab of acid at the time, but I still swear there was a light comin out of her head!

Anyway, I hope you've enjoyed the read. And if you've found it tasteless or offensive you're takin it all too seriously, pal. Life is meant to be laughed at. It's a joke, a

*Misogynist. *Charmaine*

dance, a party to which we're all invited. Just turn up, play a few games, burst a few balloons, then collect yer party bag and go home. What else you gonna do? Stay in bed and let it pass you by?

We're all gonna snuff it, every single one of us, and it won't matter what you've done or where you've bin, how much money you've made, how many birds you've nobbed, we'll all be brown bread. As Mike Tyson said: "Life isn't about what you acquire, it's about losing everything."

Like the rasters I believe that dope is the pathway to the soul. A few spliffs and your spirit soars. Well, *mine* does. I obviously don't advocado it for *everyone*. You're either a head or you're not. You either get it or you don't. You can also be a pot-head wivout ever havin a spliff. There are these cool dudes who get what life's about wivout *any* kind of drug or stimulent and live accordianly (you know who you are).

It's a dream that we're all gonna wake up from. And all there is at the end of the day is a fat load of nuffin.

EPILOG

It happens to everyone. You wake up wiv that strange eerie feelin that somefin is wrong. Somefin is missin, somefin ain't right. You don't know what it is or where it's come from. An odd mix of longin and regret. You don't know what to make of it, you're not sure what it means. It takes a while. You rack yer brains. Then – suddenly – it happens – you sus it - it hits you. And the implicashuns are *terrifyin*! *More* than terrifyin, a positive muvverfuckin, ball-brakin tsunami of the senses!

YOU'RE MISSIN YER EX!

No! This can't be happenin! Where the fuck has *this* come from? You haven't fort about her for almost a year, now suddenly you can't get her out of yer head. You're missin her big warm tits in bed at night, her hairy legs what she used to forget to shave draped all over you. You're even missin her horrible bloody kids! Ok, fings were crap before you left. She'd let herself go and she could be as irritatin as Ray Winston's Bet 365 commercials. But maybe she weren't that bad after all. Maybe if you'd bin a bit kinder, a bit more attentive, more respectful. After all, she absolutely *adored* you at the beginin. Fort you were the dog's bollocks, couldn't do enuff for you. You had minge on tap, she made you munchy snacks at night, and didn't mind you seein her on the loo. Maybe you had it pretty good wivout realisin it. And bein on yer own ain't all what it's cracked up to be. It's alright at first, then it wears a bit thin. There's only so many wanks you can have before runnin out of material. And it *does* get a bit lonely sometimes. At least wiv her you had someone to row wiv.

So what you gonna do? You could try to forget it and carry on but she keeps comin back into yer forts. You can't ring her coz she's blocked yer number, you don't even know where she is, she might have moved. Here's what *I* did.

***

I had a bath, the first one in months coz the lock's broke and you don't know who's gonna wander in for a wee - had a shave, did the barnet, got all dressed up in me best t-shirt 'n' jeans, plus me brand new Nike trainers what Rob The Knob got off the back of a lorry. If I say so myself, I looked like Brad Pitt in his heyday.

I went to Brighton station, bought a ticket to Watford and a massive bunch of flowers from the florists, somefin I'd never done before in the four years we was together. A beautiful bookay all co-ordinated and rapped up in sellerfane (40 fuckin quid they cost but they weren't 'alf nice!). And the next fing I know I'm on the train to Victoria, which is surprisinly empty for 1 o' clock on a Saturday, and I'm dead nervous, plannin what I'm gonna say to her. Tell her how sorry I am and how much I've missed her. Tell her how life just ain't bin the same wivout her. How I've realised how much she and the kids meant to me. *Then* all these doubts come in. Is this *really* what I want? Is it coz there's nuffin better on offer? Maybe I'm bein led by my dick. And what if I'm rejected? All these forts. I felt like Jesus when he went into the desert to do battle wiv Satan - unless, of course, he was an alien and simply went back to his planet for a few weeks.

I suddenly need a wee. I get up and go in. It *reeks* as only train toilets can. I lift the seat. There's half a dozen turds floatin on the top, along wiv a loada bog-roll. The flush obviously don't work coz it's almost overflowin. I mean, who has a shit on a train? What sort of moron waits till there sittin on the 12.48 to Victoria and decides to have a dump? Do they find it *excitin* or somefin?! Why didn't they go before they left? I grimace and try not to look as I undo my zip and aim it at the bowl. Suddenly, the train jerks to a halt. The piss goes everywhere, but mostly over my brand new Nikes. I quickly finish and put it away. Then, would you fuckin believe it, I get what I call 'surplus spillage'. Blokes will know what I'm talkin about. You fink you've finished, you do up yer flies, then all of a sudden yer fuckin bladder decides to carry on as if it had a life of its own and you're left wiv a massive great wet patch right near the tip of yer todger.

I return to the carriage wiv soakin wet trainers and lookin like I've pissed myself. Suddenly the train is packed! Every seat is occupied and people are standin. Of *course* .... East Croydon! All the plebs get on at East Croydon. Where the hell they all come from God only knows, but it happens every fuckin journey! It must have the population of China! And to my horror someone is sittin in my seat – a big fat woman just sittin there like she owns it.

"Excuse me," I go. "You're sittin in my seat."

She looks at me like I'm a bad smell (which I probably am).

"Got your name on it, has it?" she goes.

Then I suddenly realise she's sittin on the fuckin flowers!

I scream at her to get up.

"I've paid for this seat," she says rigidly.

"You're sittin on my bookay!"

She looks puzzled for a moment, then stands up to find it squashed beneath her enormous grotesque buttocks.

"Oh – sorry," she says unconcerned. "Didn't see it."

"No, must be difficult wiv an arse that size," I say.

She looks at me daggers and hands 'em to me. They're completely flattened!

"Forty fuckin quid they cost me!"

"So sue me."

Then she flops down again as though nuffin has happened. The bloke sittin next to her just carries on readin his paper, ignorin everyfin like people do on trains.

I make my way down the carriage and stand the rest of the way wiv everyone seeminly starin at my crutch and the enormous wet patch on my jeans.

I finally arrive at Watford just before 3. I find the high rise, go up the six floors coz the lift's broke as usual, still clutching the flowers which by now look like they've bin 12 rounds wiv The Incredible Hulk, especially since gettin stuck in the tube doors. I find the flat and ring the bell while struggling to regain my breath. I'm sweatin like a bitch, me hair's all messed up, and I've got butterflies doin the hokey-cokey in the pit of my stomach.

There's a wait. I start to fink she's not there. I'm disappointed but also, if I'm bein honest, ever so slightly relieved. I fink about leavin when all of a sudden the door opens and there she is – Delores. Lookin just like she used to – no - *better*. She's wearin makeup and her hair's all done. She's also lost a ton o' weight. In fact she looks fuckin *incredible*! And I get an instant hard-on coz she's only wearin a short silk nightie, dead posh, the like of which I'd never seen her wear before. I'd forgotten how shapely her pins were. *And* she's shaved 'em. Perhaps she had a premonition I was comin and wanted to get ready for me. I have instant visions of her takin me strait into the bedroom and gettin me to fuck the life out of her, makin up for lost time. Her face drops on seein me.

"Oh no!" she grimaces.

"It's me," I smile.

"I can see that! What do you want?"

I fink she's muckin about.

"Is that any way to greet a friend?"

"*Friend*? You're no fuckin friend! Three fuckin grand you had off me!"

"I was *desprate*!" I plead. "It ain't easy startin again, yer know!"

"Tellin everyone my fanny farts? And I've got a dangly bit what hangs out when I'm horny?!"

"Yeah, but I always fort that was attractive."

"You're an arsehole! You've always bin an arsehole and always *will* be! Now sling yer hook!"

"But I've come all this way to see yer! Over two fuckin hours it's taken me!"

Then I hand her the flowers. She stares at 'em, speechless.

"What the fuck are *these*?"

"A fat woman sat on 'em. But it's the fort what counts, right?" Then I play the hard-done-by stepdad card. "And I'd really like to see the kids."

"They're not here. They've gone to the shops wiv some older kids."

"Well, can't I come in and wait till they come back?"

She looks reluctant, finally relents, and steps aside to let me in. I go into the hall and look around wiv genuine affection.

Aah, the old place – just as I remembered it.

You could almost smell the nostalga. Then I turn back to her and give her that old lechy look that always used to get her goin.

"Lookin good, darlin," I say, rollin my shoulders confidently.

"Is that a fact?" she responds, unimpressed.

"*Very* tasty. In fact, I don't fink I've ever seen you lookin so fit."

"Yeah, there's a reason for that."

"Oh? What's that?"

"I've found someone who treats me well."

And suddenly there he is - sittin in the kitchen wiv his legs crossed like he owns the place, wearin leather slippers and some poncy dressin gown wiv the letter 'H' on the breast pocket – centre-partin and droopy mustache like somefin outa the sixties – the last fing I expected to see!

"This is Hubert," she goes.

Hubert? What sort of fuckin name is Hubert?!

"He's Belgium. We met on holiday in Spain."

Spain? When did she ever go to Spain?!

"I won ten grand on the lottery, so me and the kids went for a fortnight."

Eh? I'm trying to take all this in. *Spain, Hubert, ten grand*?!

"I decided to have horse ridin lessons and Hubert was the instructer. That's how we met." And she regards him adorinly.

I look at this fucker sittin there all cocky and full of himself and I wanna puke.

"How long's he bin here?"

"Two weeks."

"Does he speak English?"

"Yeah, *course* he does!" she says, like I'm an imberseal.

Then he stands up and holds out his hand.

"How do you do," he says in a perfect English accent. "You must be Dave, the one who blackmailed her for three thousand."

We shake hands and both sit. I'm completely befuddled, and like a total dork I say the first fing that comes into my head.

"So how was your flight?" I ask him slowly, stressin each word like I'm talkin to a retard.

"A bit noisy. I was in economy. I usually travel business class but there were no seats. I would have had to wait for a later flight and it was imperative I follow Delores and the children as soon as possible to see the kind of hovel they've been living in. I have to return in a few weeks as I'm expanding the stables, so time is of the essence."

Fuck me! The bloke spoke better English than what *I* did!

"*Own* the stables, do yer?" I ask, jealousy kickin me in the balls.

"Yes, that and the pleasure complex next door."

"You should see him on his horse!" Delores exclaims, all proud.

Is this cunt for *real*? Ridin stables *and* a pleasure complex? Good job his name's Hubert and he wears his hair like Austin Powers, uvverwise he might be a real threat.

"Would you like a joint?" he suddenly asks.

"Er .... yeah," I respond, amazed, and he opens this tin and brings out his neat fuckin rizlas, along wiv his neat fuckin roaches already cut to size, an enormous bag of grass, and proceeds to roll the neatest spliff I've ever seen in my life!

Fuckin marvellous, I fink. She never let *me* smoke in the kitchen! Reckoned it was unhigenic.

He finishes rollin it and hands it to me, politely allowin me to have the first toke. He brings out this expensive-lookin lighter from his dressin gown pocket and I light up. Fuck me, it was strong! The first hit almost blew my head off, though I tried to make out it had no effect. By the third puff, I'm completely out to lunch.

"Pretty good shit," I say, handin it back to him and tryin my best not to turn alien green.

"Acapulco Gold from Belgium. The best."

"Natch," I say, soundin strangely effeminate.

Then the door goes and Delores leaves to answer it, still in her skimpy sexy nightie. And I suddenly realise what's bin goin on. They've bin bonkin! Him and her. The dirty fuckers! They was bonkin when I arrived! That's why she didn't immediately come to the door! That's why they're still not dressed! Three o' clock on a Saturday afternoon and the filthy fuckers are at it whilst the kids ain't around! Is there no morality *left*?!

There's an awkward silence between me and him and he hands me the joint again. I try and fink of somefin to say.

"So how's the sex?" I ask.

"Highly fulfilling," he answers, wiv no sense of irony. "She gives very good blow-jobs."

EH?! She never gave *me* a blow-job! Not unless I shoved it in her mouth whilst she was yawnin!

Suddenly the kids come in. First Romeo, followed by Daisy Mae. They both looked a bit older and sort of different, better dressed and cleaner somehow. Both of 'em totally blanked me. Romeo goes strait to Hubert and I can't believe my lugholes.

"May I go and play at William's house, please, uncle Hubert? Mum says I can if you agree."

"And where does William live?" asks Hubert, all paternal.

"He's just five doors along," interjects Delores, soundin like she's mum-of-the-year.

"Then I don't see why not," says Hubert wiv kind orthority.

I stare at Romeo open-mouthed. Was this the same kid that used to torture slugs before eatin 'em? Then I look at Daisy Mae who's now five and still as sweet-lookin.

"Hello, Daisy Mae," I smile. "Remember me?"

She eyes me up and down wivout much enthusiasm.

"Yeah, you're the one she kicked out for bein a wanker," she says. Then she promptly sits on Hubert's lap and the two of 'em have a cuddle.

"May I go and play at William's as well, please, uncle Hubert?"

"Yes, but I'd like you both back by six o' clock as we're all going out for dinner."

And she snuggles into him, all coy, almost flirtin wiv him.

"Where are we goin?"

"Where would you *like* to go?"

"McDonalds!" they both shout at once.

"Then that's where we're going."

They both cheer excitedly.

"But only on the proviso that you allow me to take mummy to our favourite Italian restaurant tomorrow night while Aunty Beryl looks after you."

They both nod in agreement.

"Ok, you two," says Delores. "Off you go. And make sure you're back by five."

It was like a fuckin scene out of The Little House On The Prairie! Then the two kids go obediently out wivout so much as a backwards glance in my direction.

There's a silence. It feels awkward again. I realise I'm still puffin on the joint. I'm in the twilight zone. I hand it back to him.

"It's ok, Dave. Finish it. Would you like some to take back with you?"

I wanna shove his Belgium Acapulco Gold down his Belgium fuckin throat, but I *am* runnin a bit low so I say yes. He rises and gathers a plastic bag from one of the kitchen drawers, knowin exactly where to look. Talk about makin yerself at home! Then he puts a load of it in the bag and hands it to me.

"Cheers," I say begrudgingly, and put it in me pocket.

"I'm goin for a shower," he says to Delores.

"Ok, babe," and the two of 'em kiss, one o' them long, drawn-out 'look at us ain't we great not only are we in love but we're also bonkin every five minutes and I bet you wish *you* was as happy as us' sort of kisses what make you wanna reach for the sick-bucket. Smug fuckers! And off he goes into the bathroom for a shower. I didn't even know there *was* a shower! And now, suddenly, I'm left alone wiv Delores. There's a small, unspoken embarrassment.

"Ten grand, eh? That was lucky."

"Yeah, I've had a *lotta* luck since you fucked off," she says, matter-of-factly, and lights a fag.

Now I know I'm a bit out of it, possibly even somewhat delerius, thanks to his superior Belgium puff, but I'm still not convinced of her feelins. I fink maybe she's just doin all this to make me jealous.

"Listen .... Delores .... I know I wasn't the *best* boyfriend in the world .... I know I made mistakes .... but it's not too late. We can still start again. I've changed. I'm a different person. I've even learnt to cook. That Belgium bloke .... he's not right for you. Sittin there in his poncey dressin gown wiv the letter 'H' on it – that's not you. You need someone sexier, more rugged. A chick like you needs a bit o' rough like me."

And I start stroking her bare legs wiv every intention of goin all the way up to the old Moon River. She stares at me, agog.

"Are you kiddin me? You fink I'm gonna turn down a tall, rich, good-lookin Belgium guy for an out-of-work slimeball like you?"

I fink about it.

"Well .... like I said .... it's not too late."

"You're fuckin delushional!" she yells. "He's worth *ten* of you! He's smart, intelligent, dependable, polite, well-mannered, he pays me compliments, buys me clothes, takes me out, he's great wiv the kids ...."

I was beginin to wish I'd never spoke. But by now she's on a fuckin roll.

"He's strong, confident, knows who he is and what he wants, he's got his own business, speaks seven languages, rides horses, plays tennis, drives an open-top sports car, owns a speedboat, does oil paintin, he's good at DIY, and above all he's *faithful*!"

A moment's silence.

"Is that *all*," I found myself sayin.

"Do you *honestly* fink I'd choose *you* over him?"

By now I'm clutchin at straws.

"But does he make you *laugh*? I bet he doesn't make you laugh!"

She regards me wiv disdain.

"Neither did you!" she says, no change of expression.

"But he's got a droopy mustache! You *can't* be wiv someone whose got a droopy mustache! You'll be the laughin stock of Watford!"

"We won't be stayin in Watford," she suddenly announces, almost by-the-by.

The remark hits me like a punch in the soul. I kinda know what's comin.

"What do you mean?"

"We're goin back to Spain wiv him. He's got a big villa over there, plenty of room for all of us. Right in the middle of Marbella. Beautiful scenery and shops. It'll be great for the kids, it'll be great for me. New start."

And for the first time since she kicked me out I feel sad, *genuinely* sad that all this has happened. I nod understandinly.

"Yeah – I was pretty horrible to you."

She looks fortful.

"The worst time was wiv my sister."

"Yeah." I lower my eyes full of guilt. "How's her anal warts, by the way?"

She don't answer. But I know I hurt her deeply. And I suddenly want her to be happy, *really* happy. And suddenly it's ok. It seems right. He can give her the sort of life she's always wanted.

"If you're sure it's what you want ...." I say quietly.

"I'm sure," she says, also quiet.

"Then I wish you all the best. I hope it works out."

"It will," she assures me, all anger gone.

I nod again and rise. It's time to go, and the two of us walk to the door together.

"Thanks for the flowers," she suddenly says as we get there. And we exchange a smile. One of those old, familiar, knowin smiles that say it's bin a ruff bloody journey, a lotta bumps in the road, a few head-on collisions, but thank fuck we arrived in one piece.

"Ten grand, eh?" I muse. "Don't suppose you could lend me a few quid?"

She laughs, not quite realisin I mean it, and opens the door to show me out. I leave, knowin I'll never see her again.

Funny, innit? I used to wake up wiv her every mornin, sleep wiv her every night, shag her like I was gettin on and off a bus. And now it all seems like some distant, hazy, far-off dream that never really happened.

I took those days for granted. Now I'd give anyfin to have just one o' those days back again. My problem is I can't see what's in front of me. I can't even see one minute ahead. Which is why I have no future. And why I only want what I can't have. Like every uvver fucker on the planet. Which is why we're in such a mess. Which is why I keep puffin. And why I'll always be a pot-head.

***

So that's it. I'm sittin on the train back to Brighton, facin a lonely and uncertain future, a million mixed emotions runnin threw my head. It's bin as odd and perplexin as Ray Winston's portrayal of Henry the 8th wiv a cockney accent. But I'll survive. Whatever life throws at me, I'll *always* survive.

And what have I learnt? A lot. One: never go back. Two: opinions are like arseholes – everyone has one. Three: all wars end in peace. And four: every time I wear

Nike trainers fings seems to go tits-up. I'll be wearin cowboy boots from now on.

Lightning Source UK Ltd.
Milton Keynes UK
UKHW011821110119
335400UK00005B/744/P